A DRUG KING AND HIS DIAMOND 3

Nicole Goosby

Lock Down Publications and Ca$h
Presents

A Drug King and His Diamond 3

A Novel by *Nicole Goosby*

Nicole Goosby

Lock Down Publications
P.O. Box 870494
Mesquite, Tx 75187

Visit our website @
www.lockdownpublications.com

Copyright 2018 by A Drug King and His Diamond 3

Lock Down Publications
Like our page on Facebook: Lock Down Publications @
www.facebook.com/lockdownpublications.ldp
Cover design and layout by: **Dynasty Cover Me**
Book interior design by: **Shawn Walker**
Edited by: **Kiera Northington**

4

Stay Connected with Us!

Text **LOCKDOWN** to 22828 to stay up-to-date with new releases, sneak peaks, contests and more...
Thank you.

Submission Guideline.

Submit the first three chapters of your completed manuscript to ldpsubmissions@gmail.com, subject line: Your book's title. The manuscript must be in a .doc file and sent as an attachment. Document should be in Times New Roman, double spaced and in size 12 font. Also, provide your synopsis and full contact information. If sending multiple submissions, they must each be in a separate email.

Have a story but no way to send it electronically? You can still submit to LDP/Ca$h Presents. Send in the first three chapters, written or typed, of your completed manuscript to:

LDP: Submissions Dept
Po Box 870494
Mesquite, Tx 75187

DO NOT send original manuscript. Must be a duplicate.

Provide your synopsis and a cover letter containing your full contact information.

Thanks for considering LDP and Ca$h Presents.

ACKNOWLEDGEMENT

This book was a challenge in the course of writing it as the third part in my first book series. I thank God 1 was able to complete it. My LDP team, you rock. My son Nikolvien, you make it so easy for me to write with your funny ideas. Fatima, you have read all my books, thanks. Camp Carwells ladies, thank you for the support. Demia, words can't explain how much you mean to me. You are my rock! As for you,Cory, we are riding the rollercaoster of life together till the wheels fall off. Thanks to everyone who's been reading my books.

Nicole Goosby

PROLOGUE

Chanel McClendon had become the perfect girlfriend. She was beautiful, rich, loyal, and the most understanding person King found companionship in. It had been days since Nava Munez, his ex-fiancée, returned from the disaster-stricken state of Miami in need of more than a place to stay, a car to drive and money to fund her precarious lifestyle. Not only did Chanel agree to King's vow to help his ex-fiancée when and where he could, she also offered to assist him in the effort.

Despite being warned about Nava's real nature and having seen for herself the woman's gimmicks and excesses, Chanel continued to play her part, continued to present herself as the dumb bitch Nava had taken her to be. Chanel promised herself when all was said and done, she'd be the one standing beside her King.

She, along with Camille—her friend and mentor—knew King's heart, knew the things he did for the people he made promises to. They realized that if they didn't look out for his best interest, it would be the death of him. And now that Nava had been dealt a favorable hand by King himself, the game was about to be played without rules, in which the loser or losers would lose more than they were willing to give.

"Diamond." Chris walked into the theater room and found her lounging in front of her favorite movie.

"What's up, Chris?" Diamond turned towards him and smiled. She knew what he was about to say.

Chris frowned, twisted his lips and shook his head. "I know you ain't in here doing what I think you're doing." He walked around to where he could see her fully.

"What the hell do you want, Chris? I'm watching *Tammy*. She went back to watching her movie.

"Haven't you seen this shit enough? Every time I look up, you watching this shit." Chris snatched the remote from the armrest beside her and acted as if he was about to change it.

"Nigga, do it if you want to." Diamond closed her eyes and laughed. "If you do, you through."

She always threatened him for doing something she didn't like. But today, they had business to attend to and Camille had just pulled through the gates of the McClendon Estates. "Camille is around and I'm about to head out."

Diamond sighed, stood and followed him through the high arched hallways of the mansion. This had been the only place she found solace and not only that, Nava was back with a motive as obvious as the one she at one time had. It was where Diamond came to sit back and think. And now that her plans were about to be actuated, there was nothing left to think about.

Camille pulled alongside of Diamond's pearl Calloway Corvette and climbed out of her 911 Porsche. She peeled off her signature shades, smiled at Chris and Diamond. "Let the games begin," she said.

CHAPTER ONE

King was never the one to turn his back on a person that needed his help. Since he'd promised Nava he'd do what he could for her, he was continually being called upon. He'd already put her up in a nice, two-bedroom apartment and Diamond had even given her the convertible Pontiac Chris recently bought for Datrina. But, Nava Munez wanted more. He sighed the instant her number displayed on his phone's screen. Instead of calling her back, he made a wild U-turn and headed for her place. Since her return, she'd promised to get herself together. With his finances, time and resources, he was going to make sure that's what she did.

He'd already given her money to pay off the debt she'd accumulated in her attempt to get back to him. Knowing she'd gotten back on the drugs he pulled her from at one time, he felt it was his obligation to do so again.

He parked under the canopy of the Broad Moore Apartment complex and climbed out of his Lexus truck. He'd been a player in the drug game for years now and it had rewarded him in ways many other players envied. With money came power and with power came problems. And lately, Nava was becoming just that.

King knocked on the door twice, rang the doorbell once and after receiving no response from either, he began to think the worst. "Nava!" He walked around the building to her wood-fenced patio and peered over it. "Nava!" It was unlike her to call him and not to be there when he did show. So, he felt something wasn't right. He jumped the wooden fence and tried the patio door's handle. It opened quietly. "Nava!" He heard music that seemed to be coming from the back. The stench of weed was heavy in the air, along with a scent he didn't recognize. "Nava!"

"I'm back here, King."

King exhaled, relieved he wasn't about to find her OD'd in the apartment he was paying for. He continued to walk toward the sound of music. Sade was singing about a woman in Somalia and Nava was doing her best to make the version her own. He peeked in the bedroom. Nothing. "Where you at?"

"I'm in the bathroom, silly."

King swallowed, closed his eyes and took a deep breath. He could hear the water cascading. It was obvious she'd just stepped out of the tub and the last thing he wanted was to see her naked. "You all right?"

"Of course. Why wouldn't I be?" Nava answered from where she stood.

King stood there in the hallway, not knowing how to handle the situation he was now in. He was just about to walk back into the living area when Nava appeared before him. Where she was once as thick as his best friend, Camille, Nava was now slimmer and he knew it was because of her drug use and alcohol abuse. She'd gone back to a lifestyle that took a heavy toll on her and he really did feel sorry for her. "I knocked on the door several times and even rang the doorbell and—"

Nava walked within inches of him. She looked up at him and smiled. "You were worried, so you walked around to the patio and jumped the fence," she answered for him.

"Well, yeah. I mean—" King looked back towards the front room and when he turned back around, she was inches closer. He swallowed hard.

"You mean what?" Nava began unbuckling his belt. "It's been a while. Huh?"

"What are you doing, Nava? You know I'm with Diamond now." King took a step back, but didn't stop her.

"I'm showing you what you're missing and frankly, I don't give a damn about that Diamond bitch." She pulled him to her, stood on her toes and tried to kiss his lips.

"Nava!" King held her at arm's length, looked down at her and frowned. "You know I'm not like that, never was."

"You were supposed to marry me, King. Not that stuck-up bitch." She grabbed his hand and led him to her room. But feeling his reluctance, she told him, "I'm not going to bite you, King. You know I would never have you do anything against your wishes."

"So, what's up?"

"I was thinking about a few things and wanted your input, is all." Nava led him into her room and instead of slipping into something more appropriate, she grabbed the lotion from her nightstand and handed it to him. "Here. Do my back." Nava smiled when she saw him eye her through her vanity mirror. She knew very few men could resist her. Now that King was back in her life, she was going to do anything to make sure she was back in his also. Instead of sitting with her back to him, she slithered onto the bed, arched her back and looked back at him seductively. "You used to love it when I did this." Nava spread her legs, showing King her clean, shaven vagina.

"Are you serious, Nava?" King smiled. He did used to love when she danced for him, posed for him and did all the things she once did in the strip clubs for him. For that brief moment, he remembered the things Nava did to him. The ways she performed sexual acts and, most of all, the ways she looked at him while she did. Nava was that freak he needed her to be. Knowing she could also be that lady in the streets, she was perfect for him. But, that was then. That was before he met Chanel McClendon, the woman he now loved more than anything in the world.

"It's not going to take long. I know that bitch is going to be blowing you up sooner or later."

"She's not a bitch, Nava. She's the reason you're driving that convertible outside." King squeezed a coin-sized amount of cocoa butter lotion into his palm and massaged it into his hands. While they were on the topic, he felt this was his chance to give Nava a better understanding of the woman he now loved.

"No, you're the reason I'm driving a convertible she gave me. If only you had waited for me—"

King cut her off. "Nava, let's not go there. Please." He then began rubbing her shoulders.

Nava climbed into the center of the bed, making King do the same. "Um, do not get in my bed with your shoes on, King," she told him with raised brows.

"Nava—"

"I'm serious, Kengyon. You know I don't play that shit."

King kicked off his shoes and reluctantly followed her. He halfheartedly massaged her shoulders and back in his attempt to get it over with. There were a few things he wanted to discuss himself and now that he had her undivided attention, he felt that time was now. "I need you to respect her, Nava."

"Yeah, whatever." Nava then folded her hands under her chin and spread her legs. "Do me right, King. I haven't been rubbed down in forever." Feeling his hands along the sides of her breasts, she moaned.

King let out a sigh of exasperation. "Nava, you're tripping now." He went ahead and squeezed more lotion onto her and trailed it the way he'd done so many times before down her back, over her naked ass cheeks and down each thigh and leg. "You tripping for real now, Nava."

Nava turned her face from him and closed her eyes. "I'm not tripping yet, King. I haven't even started."

CHAPTER TWO

After learning Q was behind the money stolen out of her husband's truck, Silvia allowed her husband to move back into the home they'd shared. She convinced him to think things through as regards to the actions he felt he should take. In the course of him heading a disaster relief team slated to help repair the hurricane's aftermath, Q and another crew member were injured. As a result of not having them covered with insurance, KP was fined thirty-five thousand dollars by the state, as well as robbed of six hundred thousand dollars by his closest friend and the crewmember. The six hundred thousand dollars was the money Diamond gave him for ownership of the small company he'd built from the scratch. Without the money, he was not only in debt, but also out of a company and job. It wasn't until after he found out Diamond and Chris weren't trying to kill him, he discovered that his best friend, Q, had done something so foul. And, it was then he swore to kill him and everyone else that had something to do with it.

"I'm serious, Silvia. I can't just overlook this shit and act as if everything is all right."

"And, I'm serious when I tell you to sit your ass down and think." Silvia had been in the game for years and although she wasn't the one to handle affairs in the streets, she knew how the game was played. She was no stranger to money, murder or mayhem and now that KP needed her help more than ever, she was going to make sure his moves were the best moves. "For now, you're going to smile, laugh and forget you ever knew Q had something to do with that money being stolen."

"But, I need—"

Silvia stood, stepped into a pair of strappy sandals, grabbed her phone, purse and keys and told him, "Acting in anger will do nothing but get you fucked off and draw unnecessary heat to me. And, that's what I don't need."

KP followed his wife to their garage, hit the remote and activated their alarm system. "I still can't believe he'd do some shit like this, babe."

Silvia still hadn't told her husband of the meeting she and Q were about to have and the sex they were planning on having. She failed to tell him his best friend lied to him about being at one place, when he was really parked outside of their home, hoping she'd answer the door. When it came to his friend Q, KP didn't know him as much as he thought he did. Now that she and KP were back on better terms, Silvia felt her near-intimate experience with Q was something she needn't let her husband know.

"I don't put shit past my closest friends," Silvia said, looking back at KP. "Now, get your ass in this truck and take me to work." She chuckled. "If truth be told, Q took advantage of your naivety. And, your naivety was your undoing."

**

Ever since Chris placed himself in charge of the operation he and Diamond ran, he found himself openly discussing the idea of buying himself and Datrina a house. They'd been staying in a three-bedroom loft for a while and it was about time he made the move to a bigger and better place. After receiving their most recent shipment of two hundred kilos of cocaine, he'd been moving no less than twenty at a time and at twenty-two thousand, five-hundred dollars apiece, every transaction conducted brought in right under half a million dollars. "One forty to go, Diamond," he told her, while securing over one point three million in the rear of the Escalade he was driving.

"Don't lose my shit, nigga." Diamond was standing on the passenger's side of the truck with Camille. She'd watched Chris transfer the bulk of her earnings from the McClendon Estate in his attempt to step up her game. With all the resources she had, there was no need to keep that much cash in one place and that was why he had it distributed to different holding facilities.

"Don't you two have something else to do?" Chris said, looking from Camille to Diamond.

Diamond and Camille walked over to her Corvette and climbed in. "Yeah, follow your ass. That's what we about to do right now."

"Oh, you don't trust a nigga now?" Chris closed the rear doors of the truck and smiled at her.

"Doesn't look as if I have a choice. Does it?" Diamond nudged the gas pedal, drowning his reply with the sounds of the customized exhaust of the Calloway Corvette. She and Camille had a date that involved shopping and with over sixty thousand dollars in cash at her disposal, she was ready to do just that.

Seeing Diamond back out of the garage, Chris shot her the middle finger and went on to do the same.

Camille watched the exchange between the two and once they were on their way, she asked her. "Was there ever a thing between the two of you?"

"Me and Chris?" Diamond frowned.

"The way you two interact goes beyond friends. I guess I should I say, 'just friends.'"

Diamond shifted to third, blew past the guy standing at the security booth and checked her rearview mirror. "You sound just like Somolia's fat ass."

"Somolia. She's the one that received the new Benz, right?" Camille knew exactly who Somolia was. She was the same woman occupying most of her most trusted friend's time.

"Yep, her new boyfriend bought it for her."

"You make it sound as if she has a few," Camille said, really fishing for details.

"As surprising as it is, he's actually the only one she's dating at the moment. All she talks about is her new man and we're still yet to see him. If you ask me, I think he is a she." Diamond laughed. "Somolia is a motherfucker and has been ever since I've known her."

"I'm sure she is."

"Silvia is expanding the salons and Somolia is about to have a grand opening soon."

"Sounds as if she's moving up in the world." Camille smiled. Diamond had been opening up to her in ways she only wished she could. In ways she really wanted to.

"Them hoes scared of the game and quiet as kept, they're making exit plans and think I don't know." Diamond turned onto the on-ramp and floored the sport car, pinning both her and Camille to the seats they sat. They both checked the radar detector.

"That's something you have to respect, Diamond. No one wants to be in this life forever."

"As long as I breathe, I'm game." Seeing she'd reached over a hundred and seventy-five miles per hour, Diamond smiled. She still had some gas under her. She accelerated.

"It gets to the point where you have to start thinking not only for yourself, but for those around you, Diamond. And for some that's way too much."

"My team's pretty good at watching their steps." Diamond crossed four lanes, slid between eighteen-wheeler trailers as if they were going backward and down shifted.

"And, what steps are you going to make concerning Nava?" Camille watched her for a response.

Diamond slowed to seventy miles per hour, looked over at Camille and smiled. "Careful ones and more than that, quiet ones. King's not even going to suspect anything."

"Well, just make sure I don't miss out. I must see the look on her face when it happens. She's always thought the worst of me and I'm more than sure she's confided in King, thinking I'm conspiring against her."

"Well, this time around, it's about me and her and I assure you, she'd rather dance with a thousand wolves than fuck with a bitch like me."

Camille laughed. She finally had the one she needed. She knew Diamond to be rough around the edges but with time, she'd shape her just right. In due time, Chanel McClendon would be priceless.

Chris pulled around to the rear of the storage unit, parked and checked the area to see who might be watching him. He contemplated calling Dell about the properties they spoke of. Making up his mind, he sighed, pulled out his phone and found Dell's contact.

Dell had just ended a call with a guy he'd been dealing with for over eight months, and wasn't feeling the direction their business agreement was going. He'd already shelled out over fifty thousand dollars to them, but they were still pressuring him for more, much more at that. He was just about to phone Raymond, his friend and business associate, when his phone's ringing caused him to pause and look at it in anger. He'd said all he had to say to the guy he'd been dealing with and for him to continue calling was beginning to be something he felt needed to be addressed. Without checking to see who the caller was, he yanked up his phone and said, "Motherfucker, didn't I tell you I'd have the money?"

"Dell?"

Dell frowned. "Who is this?"

"Chris, man. Is this a bad time?"

Dell exhaled in relief before laughing. "Hey, Chris, what's up?"

"I was just getting at you about that issues we talked about."

"Oh, yeah. What's up? You and the wifey ready or what?" Dell smiled to himself. By the way Chris was talking, money was about to be spent as well as made.

"Line me something up, man. It's about that time."

"How much we talking about investing?" Dell asked, hoping it would be worth his while. He had been spending his money left and right and in the game he was in and the way he was taught, that was the last thing you did—spend your own money.

"Um, let's keep it under half a million. Can you make something happen with that?" Chris was being modest at best. He knew he could afford something more, but with this being his and Datrina's first major purchase, he didn't want to overdo it.

"I'll tell you what, Chris. Bring me half a million cash and I'm going to make sure you get the nest and the eggs." Dell laughed. "I have the perfect place for you."

"Nothing too fancy, Dell."

"There's no such thing, Chris. It's only the best for us."

Dell ended his call with Chris and actually breathed a sigh of relief. Lately things hadn't been going as planned and now that something was working in his favor, he was going to milk it for all he could. With a half a million on the way, he'd be able to get more than a few fingers out of his pocket and that was reason enough for him to make the much needed call. As soon as the guy picked up, Dell told him, "I'll have another hundred grand before the day is out."

"I'll be there," said the guy, before ending the call from his end.

Dell lowered his phone, walked over to his bar and poured himself a stiff shot of dark liquor. He downed if fully. "Ahhh. Now, all I need is for Chris to come through," he told himself before walking over and flopping down on the leather and suede section.

Chris was hoping Dell kept things small, but by the way he was talking, it was obvious he had something going on and Chris wasn't about to argue with him about matters so small. If Dell said he had something for him, it was more than likely going to be something grand, because that was really the only way Dell rolled. Dell had not long ago bought to himself a four-million-dollar home and paid well below market value and this was what he hoped Dell would be able to do for them.

After securing Diamond's money and locking up the storage, he made his way to Silvia's salon. He wanted to tell Datrina the good news, as well as let Diamond know he'd settle for something smaller than agreed on.

***

Diamond and Camille had just parked when her phone buzzed and she saw that Chris was the caller. "Let me take this right quick."

"Business before pleasure," Camille told her.

"But then, there's pleasure in doing business," Diamond shot back. "Tell me something good, Chris."

"I finally got at Dell and he's going to make something happen."

"Oh yeah?" Diamond smiled. It was about time. "I'm going to put up the rest then. That sounds good, Chris."

"Um, I told him that was all I wanted to put in it."

Diamond stopped walking. "What! That ain't going to get you shit worth having, nigga. You're a stingy motherfucker."

"This is our first major purchase, Dia—"

"Fuck that shit, Chris. You—" Diamond caught herself. "I'll handle it."

Diamond cut her phone off, pushed it into her handbag and looked over at Camille. "You ready to do some shopping? She pulled out one gold card and one platinum Visa card.

"As ready as ever."

"Oh, you're a real bitch, huh?"

"When you pick your game up, Diamond, your loads don't be as heavy."

Diamond smiled, glanced over at Camille for the second time and nodded. She definitely had some picking up to do.

***

Somolia had been sleeping in late ever since she'd gotten with Buddy. Whereas they used to meet up at the hotel in their attempt to keep things on the low, she now insisted he come to her home. He'd already bought her a brand-new Mercedes—after her other one was trashed by Q—and to show him he was the only man she was seeing, the invite became permanent.

"Rise and shine, babe." She walked into her room carrying a tray. "I hope you're hungry," she told him with a smile.

Buddy looked over the food she'd prepared and swung his legs over the edge of her king-sized bed. "All this for me?"

Somolia kissed his lips. "Breakfast and dessert," she told him before raising her apron to show him she was still naked underneath. She patted her pussy. "I'm about to jump in the shower, rinse the pussy out and when you are done with breakfast," she nodded towards her vagina, "this will be waiting."

"How about we just skip breakfast then?" Buddy laughed, reached out and slapped her on the ass.

"After all the cooking I just did? Nigga, you'd better eat all of it."

Somolia smiled to herself once she was in the bathroom. This was something she'd been wanting for herself. All of her friends had men that were either rich as hell or potentially set. She'd played her cards before and only ended up receiving gifts at times, but now that Buddy was in her bed, she wasn't about to let him get away. She didn't know too much about him, but their relationship was growing and she was more than willing to see where things went with him.

She set the water right under hot and stepped into the shower. Things had definitely been looking up for her. Somolia closed her eyes as the warm water spilled over her body. For the past week or so, Buddy had been blowing her mind sexually and she was sure her part was being done as well. She ran a hand over her swollen vagina and sucked air through her teeth. "Umm, shit," she moaned, still feeling the tingling sensation between her legs. For now, sex was what Buddy yearned for and she was giving him all of her. Every part of her. She was soaping her thick thighs and ass when she heard her phone ringing. "Shit." All she needed was for one of her exes to call and screw things up. Before she was able to step out of the shower, Buddy was walking in.

"Here you go," he told her with a mouth filled with French toast, omelet and oven potatoes.

"Hello," Somolia answered.

"I take it you're not coming in today."

Somolia looked up at Buddy. "Do I have to, Silvia?"

"You have clients that's been sitting here waiting on you, Somolia."

"Shit!" She'd forgotten all about the appointments she had for the day, for the week for that matter. The time she spent with

Buddy flew by and it was beginning to be something more than she noticed.

"Yeah, that's what I said too."

"Um, give me an hour." Somolia spun towards the water so she could rinse.

"And what am I supposed to tell these women, Somolia?"

"I don't know, Silvia. Tell them the dick got stuck or something. Make up something, girl."

"Hurry your fat ass up, tramp. And, I doubt very seriously that a dick will get stuck in your—"

Somolia ended the call before Silvia could finish. She didn't need Buddy hearing the things that was sure to fall out of her friend's mouth. "Sorry, babe, but I forgot all about them hoes."

"Maybe next time, huh?" Buddy placed her iPhone on the edge of her bathroom sink. He hadn't checked in himself and was overdue for a stop or two also.

She knelt before him and took his limp dick in her mouth. She bobbed, moaned, licked and slapped herself with his dick until it was throbbing hard. One thing Somolia knew how to do was suck a dick and with minutes to do her thing, she spit on the head of his dick repeatedly, massaged his erection with both hands and once he was good and wet, she squeezed his dick with both hands and sucked only the head as fast as she could. Three minutes later she felt him swelling, felt his dick jumping inside of her mouth. She moaned, knowing it would send him over the edge. Looking up and seeing his head back and his eyes closed, she removed her hands and took him as far as she could. She swallowed everything he gave her, milked him for more and when she was sure he was both empty and satisfied, she raised up, stuck her tongue in his mouth and began sucking on his. "Tonight, I need this dick, so get here."

"Yes, ma'am."

Somolia readied herself for the day and was more than ready for her night. With Buddy, she could be that freaky bitch in the sheets, as well as the fat bitch people knew her to be in the streets.

It had been a while since she was able to call a man her own and she wasn't about to allow that to change anytime soon.

Silvia stopped in the doorway of her office, thought about Somolia's remark about the dick getting stuck and laughed. "Ladies, Somolia is in traffic at the moment and she'll be here shortly," she lied. Since she wasn't the one to be messy, that would be something Somolia mentioned when she did show, if she showed at all.

CHAPTER THREE

Diamond and Camille walked out of the Galleria shopping mall with over twelve thousand dollars' worth of designer clothing and accessories. They already knew they pretty much had the same taste in clothing and therefore, continually approved of each other's selection. It wasn't until Diamond inquired about King's taste, did Camille frown at her.

"Are you serious?"

Diamond had the jeweler display several high-end watches and thought one of them would be a nice present for him. "Yeah, I mean, I'd like for him to have something nice.

"That watch is over twelve thousand dollars, Diamond."

Diamond tsked. "I've spent more than this on bullshit."

"I'm more than sure there's something here that will cost you much less and be just as appreciated, Diamond." Camille then began looking at the less expensive watches.

"But, I like this one," she told her before nodding at the jeweler. It was final.

"You and King with these outlandish spending habits. Both of you are made for—" Camille caught herself and smiled. "You're so much alike."

"Well, I do the same for Chris and every other person in my life. I spare no expense when it comes to the things I want."

"Likewise." Camille felt exactly where Diamond was coming from, because she'd do anything for the people in her life and if money had to be spent, she had it to spend.

Both women enjoyed several laughs during various topics as they drove. Camille laughed to herself, seeing that Diamond was worse than she was when it came to speeding. She imagined the complaints King would have once he sat in the passenger's side of whatever automobile she drove. For the past couple of weeks, she'd spent more time in Diamond's company and was really starting to like the woman she was getting to know. In many ways, they were so much alike. Then, there were instances where she felt Diamond had some learning to do. But for the most part, Diamond was beyond her years and she knew that was because of her older brother, Antonio McClendon.

"After we finish with this drop, I'm going to get King a Bentley."

"I wouldn't advise that, Diamond. Besides, he could have bought his own."

"You know how men are. They're some of the stingiest people I know."

"I believe you haven't seen the things he buys for that trifling drug addict he's obligated himself to."

"Yeah, I've noticed, but those are crumbs. Sympathy crumbs at that. I used to get Antonio the exact same way." Diamond thought about the way Nava was using King, thought of the plans she had just for her and shrugged. "It's nothing."

"One thing you must know about women like her is that she'll do anything to get what she wants."

"Then that's what we have in common. The only difference between me and that bitch is she has too many habits, too much baggage and can't see past the money. She's going to kill herself before it's over with."

Camille faced her. "You seem sure of it."

Diamond maneuvered through traffic skillfully, checked her rearview and shrugged. She told her, "At least that's what it's going to look like."

***

King knew he'd been out of pocket a little longer than he'd planned and felt it was time he returned Diamond's call. They had made plans for the night and he wanted to make sure she didn't forget. He was just about to leave Nava's apartment until he looked in her refrigerator. He closed his eyes. "Nava, where are your groceries?"

"Huh?" she asked from the hallway.

"There's nothing in the box, Nava. What have you been eating?" King closed the door and went on to look in the pantry and kitchen cabinets.

Nava walked into the kitchen with a frown that told him she didn't approve of him shaking her spot down. "What are you doing, King?" She stopped him just as he was about to look over her stove, right before he stumbled across her plate of cocaine, ecstasy pills and half-ounce of Mango Haze. The money she'd been given had been used as she saw fit and buying a bunch of groceries and the like wasn't what she wanted at the time.

"Why don't you have food in here?"

"For what, King? Better yet, for who? It's not like you're here with me. What the fuck I need all that shit for?"

King felt sorry for her. His heart broke, seeing her lack of concern for herself. "Put something on, we're going shopping."

"I don't have time for that shit, King. I have—"

"What? King pushed her on his way to her bedroom. "You don't have time for what?" He grabbed a pair of sweats, pulled one of her sweaters out of her drawer and handed them to her. "Put this on."

"I'm not wearing that, King. The shit don't even match." She pouted. She liked the way King took care of her,

"Well, find something because we're going grocery shopping." He looked around her room before walking out, leaving her standing there in her panties and bra set. He thought about the ways Camille admonished him after looking inside his refrigerator. He thought of all the times he only wanted to binge on pizza and soft drinks. King then saw himself as being to Nava what Camilla was to him. And, as for now, he had to be. "You've got ten minutes, Nava."

King walked into the living area and took a seat on the sofa he'd recently bought her and pulled out his phone. He had to call Diamond.

"Hey, you," she answered on the third ring.

King smiled. "You busy?"

"Not really, what's up?"

"Just want to make sure we on for tonight." King adjusted himself on the sofa and continued. "I've been thinking about you all day as it is."

"Really?"

"Hell yeah, really."

"I'm more than sure ya fiancée is entertaining enough to the point where I'm not at the top of your thoughts."

"Diamond." King sighed. "You are the only woman for me and you know this. If you want me to leave here, I will. Just say the word."

Nava walked into the living room and modeled her outfit for him. "How do I look?"

King quietly nodded and went back to talking to Diamond. "You hear me?"

"Do what you do, King. You made her your responsibility, so deal with it. I'm not tripping on her."

"Thanks, babe. See, this is why I love you. You have the biggest heart, Diamond."

"Yeah, well, just make sure you don't forget we have plans for tonight."

"Never."

"I'll talk to you then."

King lowered his phone with a wide smile on his face. He was going to make sure she understood and knew just how much she meant to him later that night. And, if all went according to plan, it would definitely be a night she remembered.

He looked up to see Nava standing beside the sofa with both her hands on her hips. "What?"

"So, you're just going to disrespect me like that, King?" She walked around and stood directly in front of him. "That's how you going to do me?"

"Nava, you tripping. You know about her and she knows about you."

"You get at her on your own time, King. While you're with me, you cancel that bitch, or I will."

"Are you ready or what?" King looked over her attire and exhaled. She wasn't exactly on the same level with Camille or even Diamond for that matter, but she had dressed in something better than she had been wearing.

"I'm serious, King," she said before grabbing her phone and handbag. "Y'all ain't that damn close."

***

Diamond fingered the buttons on her steer wheel, ending the call with King. She looked over at Camille and smiled. "I have the biggest heart," she said proudly.

Camille laughed. "So, it would seem."

"And instead of the bitch quiet, she just had to make her presence known. This bitch is so small."

"Not to mention, shallow," Camille added.

"Shallow as hell."

***

Datrina and Silvia could only listen and shake their heads, once Somolia got to explaining and justifying all and everything she did. She'd been telling them how she'd been catering to her man and her rewards for doing so. She was even able to point to her brand-new Mercedes to prove it.

"That's too much information, Somolia," Datrina told her, hearing how her friend spoiled her man with the ass. Literally.

"Well, I'm just telling y'all what time it is. Niggas be acting like they don't want no ass, but as soon as they see you cleaning that motherfucker out, they dicks start smiling."

"You're sick, Somolia," said one of the women present.

"Go home and let your man see you cleaning your ass out and see what he does. I'm telling you."

"Somolia, will you please find something else to talk about?" Silvia asked, having heard enough.

"And, you know what I'm talking about, Silvia. KP's stretched your asshole—"

"Somolia!" Silvia yelled, not wanting to be a part of the conversation they seemed to be interested in.

"I mean—" one woman began, seeing it being something she wanted to know about. "How exactly is that done?"

"You've got to let him finger you first. Get that ass good and wet. Then—"

Datrina stopped her before she could get started. "She's talking about cleaning it, Somolia. Your fat ass just can't help it, can you?"

"All I have to say is that if you don't, some other bitch will." Somolia twisted her lips before continuing with her client. It was simple as that and they all knew it.

"I guess that would be the case when your man's with you for the things you do and allow him to do, instead of being with you for the person you are," said Datrina, seeing some of the other women look as if they were taking Somolia's statement to heart.

"I don't see anything wrong with it, I just don't want that to be the deal breaker when it comes to my relationship," one woman told the bunch of them.

Somolia walked around to were Datrina stood and told them, "I'll be damned if that becomes a dealbreaker, when a nigga spending damn near one hundred thousand dollars for it."

"Ain't that the truth!" said another woman.

"You'd better learn how to lubricate that motherfucker and act as if your world didn't turn unless he did fuck you in the—"

"Som—" Silvia hurried to place her hand over Somolia's mouth. They all knew the subject and having her go there wasn't needed. At all.

***

It had been a couple of days since KP moved back into the home he and his wife shared. With what he found out about his friend, he didn't plan on doing something rash in terms of murdering the dude, except if murder was inevitable. He pulled behind Q's Audi and parked. For now, he was going to play it the way his wife instructed him to. At least, that's what he was hoping.

Q was stepping out of the shower when his doorbell startled him. He'd been on edge for the past week. The last person he wanted to deal with right now was the guy he'd just opened his door to. "KP?"

"Yeah, nigga. What's up?" KP pushed past Q and made his way to the kitchen. Something he'd always done.

"Where you coming from, nigga?"

"I had to drop Silvia off at work." KP opened Q's refrigerator. "Damn, nigga, what's all this beer and shit for?" KP couldn't help but frown. It looked as if a party was about to happen.

"Um, I went ahead and stocked up while I was at the store."

"Ah, yeah?" KP grabbed a couple of the bottles, pulled out the chair to the kitchen table and took a seat. "Where you headed?"

"I got a job lined up. It ain't shit though." Q shrugged.

KP took a long swig before slamming the bottle down on the glass table. He knew that would definitely get a reaction out of his friend and when he didn't, he continued his questioning. "Why you didn't call me? You know I need some work right now."

"Man, I figured you'd be wanting to spend some time with your wife, being that you two just reconciled."

KP watched him as went back into his room. He looked around at the brand new appliances and furniture. It was obvious he'd been spending the money Jeff gave him,money stolen out of KP's truck.

"Your insurance company already got at you or what?" KP asked from where he sat.

"Huh?" Q appeared in the entryway, while pulling his shirt over his head.

"I see all this new shit and thought about the insurance policy you had on your house."

"Oh,yeah.Them hoes ain't finished paying me yet though."

KP nodded. "Bleed them hoes, man."

"You already know what it is, nigga." Q laughed, the humor of it not felt.

"Well, let me bend a few corners right quick. I have a few stops to make for Silvia."

"She already got you putting in work, huh?"

KP stopped.If his friend only knew it was Silvia that kept him from actually doing just that. "You don't even know the half."

KP made a couple of blocks and parked at the top of the street. He knew Q was about to meet with Jeff, but he wanted to see for himself. He wanted to make sure it was really the way it seemed when it came to his best friend and the things he did behind his back. He waited for about twenty minutes, before spotting Q's Audi pull up at the top of the street and head in the direction of Jeff's house. He thought about the relationship they had over the years. Now wondering what other things Q might have done behind his back, it was then he thought about his wife and the ways they treated each other at times. "Hell, naw!"

***

Dell had been expecting Chris to arrive for the past couple of hours, but looking towards the bottom of his stairs at the guy that just pulled up, his mood immediately changed. Chris was to deliver money needed to pay off a couple of people and with him still not showing, it would be money he had to come out of pocket with.

"I'm glad you came around, Dell," the guy told him as soon as he climbed out of the unmarked car.

"Um, it's not here yet." Dell placed both his hands in his pockets and looked down at the guy as he climbed his stairs.

"Come on now, Dell. We've been through this too many times, man."

Dell exhaled, looked towards the entrance on his estate and closed his eyes. Chris had never lied to him or put him in any game and knowing this. He led the guy into his home, offered him a drink and told him, "Give me a few minutes." He'd just have to take his money out of the cash Chris was about to deliver. He was unlatching the clamps to his piano safe when his phone rang. That had to be Chris. "Talk to me, Chris."

"Not Chris, but Diamond."

Dell rolled his eyes upward. "What's up, Diamond?"

"Chris told me he got at you about looking into a couple of properties."

Dell smiled. "Yeah, I have a couple in mind."

"Well, fuck that shit. I want them to have the house by the old Firestone," she told him, referring to the fairly new property that had been foreclosed on. The million-dollar property was only five minutes from where she lived.

"Are you talking about the one with the property in Irving? The six-bedroom home with the built-in gym and pool?"

"Yeah, yeah."

"Chris told me he wanted to keep it under a hair a—"

"That nigga ain't talking about shit. This isn't for him, it's for Datrina and I want her to have that house."

"That home isn't with either of the agencies I deal with, Diamond. He'd actually have to pay pretty much the entire asking price."

"And?"

"And that means he'll have to put up more than half a million." Dell began pulling stacks of bills from his piano safe and placing them into a medium duffel.

"Then put the rest out. A quarter million ain't going to hurt y'all and I'm more than sure if you pull up with that much cash, the deal would be done."

"I don't know about that, Dia—"

She cut him off. "I already talked to Antonio and he told me to tell you to make it happen. Call me when you do, so I can be the one to surprise both of them."

Dell threw his phone across the room and slammed shut his piano lid.

This wasn't a part of the play he put in motion and for her to go behind his back and consult with Antonio about these matters, only proved what he'd been telling his partner, Raymond, for the longest. Diamond was not only given too much power, but she was actually digging into their pockets daily.

There was no way he could tell Antonio he wasn't about to put up the money for Datrina and Chris' new home. Hell, he was counted on for times such as these and now that he'd been summoned by the boss, he had to show up.

CHAPTER FOUR

Raymond was feeling pretty good about himself, even before holding the investors' conference and now that he'd welcomed several new investors to their team, his confidence had soared. Along with them came both money and opportunity and looking at the projections he came up with, they'd be looking at returns sooner than expected, and the Circle would be looking at figures also. He shook several hands, got complimented on a job well done, and had just climbed into his Rolls Royce when his cell phone began vibrating. He'd sent Dell to voicemail twice already, because not only was Dell scheduled to do a presentation, but he wasn't answering his phone when Raymond called. It was only fair. Now that the meeting was over, Raymond had a few choice words for his friend and business associate. "What do you want, Dell? You were supposed to be here, man."

"Some shit came up and I had to deal with it. How'd it go? You get more investors or what? How much we playing with?" Dell asked successively.

"The shit fell apart, Dell. I was depending on you to bring it home," Raymond lied. There was use in telling Dell of the good news when he was suspect as it was and after consulting with Silvia, Raymond felt it was in the best interest of the investors that he dealt with their money. "Being that you knew the numbers, you would have been able to see them where I couldn't," Raymond went on to explain.

"God dammit, Raymond. We needed those investors, man."

"You should have shown up, Dell. I was—"

"I told you something came up and I had to take care of it. You've been doing this shit for years. You still can't do shit without me."

"Excuse me?" Raymond knew he didn't just hear those words.

"You couldn't hold down a little meeting?"

"Hold up, Dell. Hold up," Raymond told him before pushing himself back in the plush seat of the Rolls Royce. He peeled off his glasses and rubbed the bridge of his nose and continued. "Motherfucker, I'm the one holding this shit together. Every time it's time to do real business, you choose to go missing and come back, talking about some shit came up. I'm the one out here trying to get motherfuckers to invest in shit they can't see, nigga. I'm the one trying to make us money, not spend it."

"Yeah, well fuck all that shit 'cause we're about to have to spend more anyway."

"What, what you mean, spend some more?"

"Chris wants to buy a house for him and Datrina—"

"Okay, and?"

"Motherfucker, can I finish?"

Raymond sighed. "Yeah, go ahead."

"Anyway, Chris told me to keep things under half a mil and he was supposed to bring me that. Then, I got a call from Diamond's power-struck ass and now we about to shell out another half a million on that purchase."

"Well, Datrina is a part of what we have going on and it's only fair that we meet them halfway, on whatever they decide to do or buy, for that matter."

"This bitch is playing us, Raymond."

"Who?"

"Diamond, that's who, and you can't even see it."

Raymond shook his head in disbelief. "She just looking out for members of our team, Dell. I can see if the woman done went off and bought a warehouse filled with bullshit but she's not. She spends her money on her, our money on us and our investors' money on them. Where is this problem?"

"Don't say I didn't warn you, Raymond. We go broke, that's on you."

"You're tripping, Dell. Get some rest."

"That's on you, nigga."

Raymond ended the call before Dell could start in again. Hoping he'd be able to get a better hold on the situation and a better angle to look at things from, he decided to call Silvia.

Despite her request to be left out of the day to day when it came to them, he still needed her input. Always did.

***

Silvia was filing a few papers when Raymond's call came. She scanned the parking lot from her office window, because she didn't want KP accidentally walking in on their conversation. After telling him that she was through with the Circle, his finding out otherwise would definitely be looked at in ways she didn't feel like explaining. Knowing KP would be there shortly, she answered.

"Tell me something good, Raymond."

"We have a problem."

"We?" Silvia's brow raised.

"Yeah, we. You got a minute?"

She could tell by the tone of his voice that he needed to both talk and vent, and as many times as he was there for her, she wasn't about to turn her back or ear on her friend. "Yeah, I guess so."

"I know you said you're through, Silvia, but I need you this one time. I just got off the phone with Dell and—"

"Dell?" she asked, cutting him off.

"Yeah, Dell. He's tripping on the fact that Diamond is insisting on us matching Chris on his house purchase."

"How much is it, Raymond?"

"No more than half a million."

Silvia tsked. "That's it?"

"Yeah, he's acting as if it's pulling his drawers all the way in his ass too."

"I thought you said there was right at seven-million in cash at the ready?"

"The last time we went over the books it was, but Dell went and put some funds elsewhere and there hasn't been a return on that. Then, we had to spend more money on the salon we're about to open and—"

"That venture isn't costing us anywhere near a million and matching Chris with the purchase of their home isn't either. I can see if you were buying the house for them. I feel as if it's a worthwhile investment. They can rent out the loft for two thousand dollars a month easily and that's for-sure money."

"That's the way I see it also. He's really tripping on the fact that Diamond is pushing the pieces."

"Regardless of whose idea it is, she just as much a part of that Circle as either of you and she has that right."

"Hey, I'm not tripping on her like that. As long as she continues to bring in money, I'm not tripping."

"Then, it's final. He's to match Chris's dollar amount and if he has ties with the realtors owning the property, it's a win-win. Right?"

"That's the way I see it also. I'm going to get back at Dell and get that taken care of."

"Call me if you need anything." Silvia pressed end and placed both her elbows on her glass desk. The more she wanted out, the more they pulled her in. She did like the fact that Diamond was looking out for her closest friends, but she also knew the ego was at play. Where they kept her out the Circle because of her inexperience, she was now showing them her capabilities, both inside and out. Silvia knew how Diamond was and when it came to her right-hand, Chris, she wasn't about to take no for an answer. There were to play the game player to player, and since Diamond was now a major player in the game Silvia had played for years, she had a little piece of advice for her. Advice she was hoping she heeded to.

***

Both Diamond and Camille were sitting watching an action-packed movie in her theater room, when her phone summoned her and instead of taking the call there and disturbing Camille, she stood and walked out. She made her way to the kitchen. "What's up, cousin?"

"You busy or what?"

"Yep, got company," Diamond said, hoping it would shorten the call and allow her to go back towards the action movie she was watching.

"Well, put a pause on that shit. We have more pressing issues to discuss."

Diamond rolled her eyes upward and walked out onto her spacious patio. "What's up?"

"I heard you're pushing Dell's buttons."

"Pushing his buttons? All I did was tell him what I expected out of him."

"And, what was that, Diamond?"

"I want Datrina and Chris to have something nice and since he's been making all this noise about the moves he makes, I need for him to do just that for them."

"What you're really doing is flexing your muscle. They've been working for your brother and now you feel entitled."

"It has nothing to do with what I feel entitled to, Silvia. It's the right thing to do. You already know Antonio would see it that same way so therefore, I saw no wrong in it."

"There's ways to get things done, Diamond, and you need to learn how to approach those guys you're continually dealing with. Their egos are as big as yours and you see what happens when they collide. Dell is feeling some type of way with you calling shots."

"He's feeling what type of way? I just want him to take care of his business, instead of talking about it. That nigga tripping over me calling shots, then he needs to start making the money move. And, matter of fact, I think Chris needs a new truck and the Circle is going to buy it. How about that?"

"Diamond, listen. You continually swinging your dick, so to speak, in their faces ain't going to smooth things over. You're still a woman in this male-dominated business and you'll always be looked at as such."

"Correction, I'm that boss bitch dominating these niggas in this business and now that a motherfucker thinks I'm the one up in his shit, I'm about to show how dirty I can get."

"Think about your moves before—"

Diamond cut her off. "Fuck Dell. He ain't seen me move yet." Diamond pushed the end call button and immediately scrolled her phone for Dell's contact. It was time she told him what she would and wouldn't allow, and him running to her cousin was a roundabout way of snitching, and that was something she wasn't about to deal with.

***

Silvia covered her face with both hands. Instead of clipping the stem to either of the bombs she stood before, she'd only ignited them and there was definitely about to be an explosion, if not some. When looking at the things happening around her, she couldn't seem to find an end. If it wasn't Dell, it was Diamond and when it wasn't either of them, it was KP and Somolia. There was always something going on and when thinking about it, she was dead center of it all. Silvia needed her cousin badly. She needed Antonio McClendon out.

***

Q pulled in front of Jeff's home just as he was heading out. He'd been thinking things through and had a favorable proposition for his new friend.

"I was hoping I'd catch up with you before you left," he told him.

"Yeah, what's up?"

Q walked over to Jeff's recently-bought Dually and climbed into the passenger's seat, indicating that he was about ride with him. "You know I have KP's old contacts, right? The way I see it, if I was to become part-owner, I'll make sure we keep work and I'm also familiar with regulations."

"So, you want half of my shit?"

"Not half. You keep sixty percent and I get forty percent. It's a win-win for both of us."

"What about KP?"

"What about him?" Q frowned.

"Is he coming on too?"

"Naw, he's doing his own thing." Q lied about many things, but there was some truth to his words. A truth he knew little about.

"You've got to make sure we got nice contracts, Q. Just the way you and KP used to get."

"Deal." Q held out his hand and when Jeff did the same, he smiled. He was now a co-owner and that was something KP wasn't about to hand over. When negotiating the contracts, Q was sure he'd get his cut off the top and this was enough for him to forget the way he'd wronged his best friend. Business was business.

***

After following Q to Jeff's and seeing him climb into the truck with him, KP headed to the Totally Awesome Salon to see if his wife was ready. He did want to listen to his wife, but here Q was, playing against him and it was something he was having a harder time dealing with. It was obvious money had been spent, split and made, and the bond they all once shared had shattered. And, it was now that he needed to take matters into his own hands. He called the one person he knew could help him with the dilemma. He phoned Chris.

***

Chris fondled Datrina playfully while she straightened her station for her next client. He'd been touchy-feely ever since his arrival and knowing how Somolia liked to keep their names and the nature of their relationship in the air, he made it known she was the only woman for him and he had a surprise for her. "I'm serious this time, babe."

"Yeah, whatever, Chris."Datrina pushed past him and headed to the supply closet.

"What's the surprise, Chris?" Somolia asked as soon as they were out of Datrina's hearing.

"It's big, Somolia. Real big."

Somolia twisted her lips. "You said that the last time. Remember?"

"Just see it like this. Diamond felt I was being cheap when I told her I only wanted to spend half a million." Chris winked at her.

Somolia stopped and faced him. "You're buying her a house, Chris?" He nodded and smiled.

"Where?"

"That's the question I can't answer, Somolia. Dell is looking into it as we speak."

"It's about time, Nigga. You've been having my girl in that damn apartment for too long."

Seeing Datrina round the corner with her hands full Chris shushed Somolia. He pulled out his phone as soon as it began vibrating and frowned, seeing KP's contact. "Somolia, that's between us," he told her, before making his way to Silvia's office. "What's up, KP?"

"Where you at, man?"

Chris looked up at Silvia and seeing her gesture that he wasn't with her, he told him, "Oh my way to the salon, what's up?"

"I need a gun, Chris."

"For what?"

"I'm going to put in some work and I need you to help me, man."

"Hold up, KP. You can't make moves like that without calculating your steps. Have you thought about what you're about to do?"

"Yep, and I need you to help me."

"And, what am I to do, besides become a witness against you, KP?"

"You don't have to do nothing like that, Chris, I just need for you to tell me how to do it. I know you be killing niggas all the time, Silvia told me."

Chris looked over at Silvia and seeing her close her eyes and shake her head, he knew it was something she told him in confidence and if KP freely gave that information up, there was no telling what else he'd willing offered up. "Who are you trying to kill, KP?"

"Q and that nigga, Jeff. They plotted all this shit against me in the first place and Q's been fucking Silvia right under my nose."

"He what?" Chris couldn't believe it.

"Yeah, I had to sit back and look at the shit. They been fucking around, man, and I can prove it."

"Okay, listen to me, KP, just chill. We'll put something together, man. But, you have to promise me that you chill for right now. I have a lot of shit going on and I can't fuck with you right now. Okay?"

"How long is it going to take then, cause I—"

Chris stopped him. "KP, it might take a year, nigga. I said, chill out right now. Go about your days and nights as if everything's good. Never let a motherfucker see you coming." Chris knew if he didn't plant some game under KP, then he'd more than likely do something stupid and none of them needed that.

"All right, all right. I got you. Don't tell Silvia shit, man."

Chris lowered his head and told him, "You'll tell before I will."

Silvia shook her head and told him, "I can't keep doing this shit, Chris. I can't." Tears formed in the corners of her eyes as Chris rushed to her side. "I want to be through with all this shit, Chris. I thought I was already through." Silvia banged her hand on her desk.

Chris caught her hand before she could act out. He pulled her to him and squeezed her. Comforted her and assured her. "Shh, I got you, Silvia. I got it now." He rocked her as she began to sob. "I got you now, Silvia." He whispered, "I promise."

As soon as KP pulled into Totally Awesome Salon's parking lot, he saw Chris waving him over and before he could put the truck in park, Chris jumped in. "When did you get here?"

"Drive."

"Huh?"

"I said drive, nigga!"

KP pulled out of the lot and made the block. He was hoping Chris had come up with a plan. "Where we headed?"

"What the fuck is wrong with you?" asked Chris.

"What—"

Chris threw the rolling truck in park, burning the transmission and grinding the gears.

"Man, what the hell is the matter with—"

Before KP could finish the words, Chris grabbed him by the throat and pinned him to the captain chair of the Escalade. He got within inches of his face and told him, "You, nigga. You're what's wrong with me and I'm tired of it."

KP grabbed at Chris's wrist while gasping for air. "Man,you,trip—."

Chris freed him, pulled his Glock with lightning speed and pressed the barrel against KP's right eye. "I'll blow your fucking brains out and won't think twice about this shit, nigga, and the reason it hasn't been down already is because of Silvia. When you do stupid shit, it falls back on her and the shit you're planning is just that—stupid."

"Okay. Come on, Chris."

"Don't bullshit me, KP. If I ever hear you talking like this, I'll burn your bitch ass. You hear me?"

"Yeah, man. Yeah. What the fuck did I do now? I thought you was—"

"I am. We will not talk about this shit anymore and you will not tell Silvia shit that's happened here or anywhere for that matter. And, when you make it back to the shop you're going act as the best husband she could have. You're going to tell her how much you love her. How glad you are that she's willing to be a part of your weak-ass life. From here on out, you're going to blow her mind and whatever she wants, you're going to do." Chris pressed the barrel into his cheek harder. "If she wants to stick her fingers in your ass, you're going to raise both legs, lick your lips and act like you've been doing the shit forever. If I even think I hear a complaint come from her, your ass is going to come up missing. We straight on that or what?

"Yeah, yeah. I'm good, man. I'm good."

Chris leaned away from KP, pushed his Glock into his waist band and said, "The way you out here acting, it's no wonder she's always running to other motherfuckers."

"I'm sorry, man. Damn."

"I'm telling you, KP." Chris smiled, making sure KP understood how the consequence would go.

"I promise, Chris, I'm good."

Chris straightened his shit, leaned away from KP until his right elbow rested on the door's arm rest and said, "Now, tell me about this shit you got going on with Q."

KP's eyes never left the view the windshield offered. He was not about to go there with Chris again and even if he was being sincere, he wasn't about to find out. As far as he was concerned, he didn't even know anyone named Q. "Who?"

Chris looked out of the passenger's window. He whispered, "That's what I thought."

Nicole Goosby

CHAPTER FIVE

Since they were doing the shopping thing, Nava made sure to select the things she knew King liked. She'd even promised him a couple of home-cooked meals. Meals she knew he loved at one time. Not only did they walk out of Super Walmart with over five hundred dollars' worth of groceries, toiletries and women's hygiene products, he also gave her two thousand dollars so she could support herself until she found something to do and this was when he brought up the things she knew so much about.

They'd just climbed into his Lexus truck when she faced him and said, "I want to manage a strip club, King."

"You want to do what?"

"A strip club. I want to manage one."

"Come on now, Nava. You're supposed to be leaving that shit alone."

Nava pouted. "I can't."

King closed his eyes and lowered his head. "What happened to all those job interviews, Nava? I'm sure there's something else you can be doing. I don't want you around all them drugs, them thugs, that alcohol and all the drama that comes with them."

"You want me to be like that bougie-ass bitch you're with? Fuck that hoe, King. That bitch just with you because of your money. Hell, I'm the go-getter, King."

"I'm not going there with you, Nava. I'm trying to help you have something and putting you up in some strip club, defeats the purpose of me trying to take you out of them."

"You're not my man, King. You're running around after that stuck-up bitch and she's got your nose wide open. This is our chance to make some major paper—something that bitch don't know nothing about. But, you brushing me off like I don't know how to take care of my business."

"What the hell you want me to do, Nava? I don't run no strip club. I don't even know anyone who does."

"Buy one, King. Front me enough so I can get a building and I'll take care of the rest."

He watched her incredulously. "Are you serious, Nava?"

"Hell, yeah. I'll have that bitch up and running in no time."

"I'm not buying any strip club, Nava. There's no way."

Nava folded her arms. "But, you go out and buy that bitch a car worth one hundred thousand dollars as if you've known her forever."

"Nava, I—"

"You don't love me, King. You never did and now I'm seeing that."

Before he could say anything in response, she told him, "Take me home, Kengyon."

Before he was able to leave her apartment, Nava ran and jumped into his arms. She knew he hated seeing her cry and she was about to use that to her advantage. She kissed his cheek and neck and pressed her face on his chest.

"I never stopped loving you, King."

King walked out of Nava's apartment, thinking about some of the things they talked about. He did want to help Nava, but he wasn't about to open a strip club just to do so. If only she'd said anything else besides a strip club, he'd have her back. He didn't care about the money, but if truth be told, he did still care about Nava Munez.

He glanced up at her bay window and noticed her watching him as he pulled away from the curb, her words replaying themselves aloud. "I never stopped loving you, King." Seeing her defeated in such a way broke his heart, but he'd moved on and when thinking about the night he had planned for Diamond it caused him to smile. He hit the on-ramp and headed to the first Jared Jewelry Store he found. And, with over twenty thousand dollars in his possession at the time, he was about to surprise her with something nice. Real nice.

***

After feeling the experience in the theater room, Camille swore she'd have one before the year was out. It was just something about the McClendon home that made people want bigger and better. "Well, we need to do this again real soon," Diamond told Camille as she gathered her clutch purse and phone.

"I'm loving this place, Diamond. I really am." Camille smiled, following her through marble hallways and lavish living areas, the eight-chair theater being her favorite so far.

"It's all right. I've seen better though." Diamond remembered her time spent in Miami at Sergio's estate. "Much better."

"I still don't think King's ready to visit. Especially now that Nava's in the picture. In his carelessness, he's bound to slip and you don't need his mistakes costing you."

Diamond thought about the way Camille saw the game. She was yet to lead her astray and with King insisting on obligating himself to Nava, there were certain things she could and couldn't allow him to do. "Yeah, you're right. I'll just insist on me driving. He likes when I drive."

Camille laughed. "He told you that?"

"Kind of."

"He lied." Camille walked over to her Porsche and climbed in. "Anything over one hundred miles per hour definitely takes away any excitement he pretends to show."

"Is that right?" Diamond tried to remember the last time she'd broken speed limits with King riding shotgun. She smiled to herself.

"I'll see you this weekend, Chanel."

Diamond watched as Camille pulled out and headed up their drive. There was definitely a woman she could see herself being with. There was only one thing Diamond felt needed changing when it came to Camille and she was about to see just what she could do about it. "Yeah, I'll see you this weekend," she mumbled to no one.

***

By the time they made it back to the salon, KP was carrying helium-filled balloons, a huge bear with several "I LUV YOU" cards and a bag filled with chocolate candies. Entering the salon, all eyes feasted on him.

"Damn, nigga, what you do now?" Somolia asked, before any of the women could. She watched Chris walk past her and snuggle up to Datrina. She looked back at KP and pointed. "All that shit's for Silvia?"

"Yes, it is, Somolia. You're acting like I don't do good shit for my wife or something."

"Yeah, only after you've fucked up something."

"Whatever." He walked past Somolia and the rest of the onlookers and headed for his wife's office.

As bad as her day was going, Silvia found humor in seeing KP enter her office with his arms filled with gifts. She laughed even harder, seeing him smile.

"Hey, babe." KP sat the huge bear on the floor beside her and placed the cards and candy on her desk. He handed her the balloons. "Here."

"Really, KP?"

"What?"

"Am I supposed to be getting well or something?" Silvia looked from the card to her husband then back to the cards on her desk. She opened the first, saw the one-hundred-dollar bill and laughed 'til tears filled her eyes.

"These are just because I know you've been dealing with a lot and tonight I'm going to make you forget about everything."

She leaned back and searched him with a dubious expression. "Really?"

"Yep, really. Tonight, it's all about you and the things you want to do, babe."

"No, the things *we* want to do," Silvia said in a yelp of delight.

Chris entered her office, along with Datrina and Somolia. The urgency they'd heard in Silvia's voice called for nothing less. "Girl, why you in here screaming?" Somolia asked, before looking up at KP.

"What brings you'all in here?" Silvia asked the trio.

"What's up, Silvia?" Chris asked, knowing no one was about to go anywhere until they were sure she and KP weren't fighting.

"Chris, you got something to do with all this shit KP dragged in here?" Datrina asked.

Chris cast Datrina a glance. "What gives you that impression?"

Somolia responded, "Because, every time you threaten his ass, he starts doing shit like this."

"He wanted to know the best place to buy these kinds of gifts and I showed him, that's all."

Silvia, Datrina and Somolia laughed at the same time. It was that obvious.

"What?" said Chris.

"Get out. Everybody get out of my office. I need to speak with my husband right quick."

Silvia waited until everyone was gone and told her husband, "Thanks, Kevin." She stood, walked around her desk and hugged him. "Thanks."

"I'm here for you, Silvia. I know I've been burying you under my shit and I apologize for that. I really do, and tonight—" He squeezed his wife, licked her neck and ear lobe then finished, "—it's all about you. Whatever you want, wherever you want to go and whatever you want to do. It's all about you." Hoping he was convincing enough, he sucked his wife's bottom lip, ran his hand between her legs and told her, "This is mine tonight."

Silvia felt something she hadn't felt in a long time and she didn't know whether to call Chris back in and thank him, or just let things unfold themselves. But, what she did know was that she was more than ready and if nothing else, she'd enjoy it.

Later that night

Since Diamond was the one insisting she drive, it was settled that she'd pick him up at his apartment and then, they'd carry out their date. It had been a minute since their schedule permitted such an event and King was looking forward to the time he was about to spend with his woman.

He was standing curbside when she pulled up. Instead of allowing her to park, he jumped in, leaned overand kissed her lips. "I've been thinking about doing that all day, Diamond."

"After a day spent with your little girlfriend, that's all you got for me?" The words flew from Diamond's mouth before she realized. She'd played the guilt card on both Antonio and Chris and seeing King dig into his pocket, she was hoping it would be worth her while.

"As a matter of fact, I do have something for you." While at the jeweler, King looked at several necklaces and pendants, but the ones that stood out the most,were the diamond choker and the heart-shaped, chocolate diamond pendant that was surrounded by eighteen-carat diamonds. He held it in front of her before placing it around her neck.

Diamond was at a loss for words. No man had ever given her anything like that before. "You're trying to get some pussy for real, huh?"

"I just wanted to get my girl something nice, is all."

Diamond checked herself in the rearview and when seeing the many colors sparkle before her, she faced him. "Yep, you trying to fuck something, King."

"I'm not pressuring you, Diamond, and that's not why I got you that necklace anyway."

"Well," Diamond leaned across him and opened her glove compartment, pulled out the box and handed it to him, "hopefully, this will change your mind about pressuring me."

King opened the box and shook his head. "You're definitely not the one to be outdone, are you?" He leaned over and kissed her again. "Thanks, Diamond." King then pulled his watch off and replaced it with the rose gold Bulova she bought for him. "I love you, Diamond."

Diamond pulled off, thinking about the many conversations she'd had with Somolia. She might not have been known to suck dick like Somolia, but tonight she was definitely going to see if her methods were true. It had been a while since she'd been penetrated by a real dick and she was about to make that happen. "We're going to get a room tonight, or what?" she asked him, knowing it was normally what the guy inquired about.

"Hell, yeah. If that's what you want to do." King reached over and squeezed her thigh. He slightly raised the Gucci mini-dress she wore.

"I don't plan on using a vibrator tonight, so I guess so." Diamond smiled to herself. It was just that morning Chris damn near caught her doing just that. "I want to feel you inside me, King."

King had never touched her inappropriately, but he was thinking of ways to do so and had been for the longest. Just as he was about to respond to her, his phone chimed. He started to ignore it until he thought about the fact that he hadn't heard from Camille since earlier today.

"Business?"

He exhaled and told her. "It's Nava."

"So, what do you need me to do?"

King dialed her number and as soon as she answered the phone, he asked her, "What is it, Nava?"

"There's a couple of guys outside that keep knocking on my door, King."

"Who are they?"

"The hell if I know. I'm scared, King. What if they—"

King closed his eyes and sighed before cutting her off. "No one's going to bother you, Nava. Cops live all over that complex. You're good."

"I'm scared, King, and I don't have anyone else to call."

"I'm in the middle of something, Nava. I—"

"I need you, King."

Diamond knew the card Nava was playing and since this would only add to the perception Nava had of her, she glanced over at King and asked, "Where does she live, King?"

"Really, Diamond?"

"It's apparent she's scared, King. After we check up on her, then we'll do what we planned on doing. It shouldn't take that long."

King smiled, reached over and squeezed Diamond's thigh and told her, "You're the best, babe."

"Anything for my man," she told him, before taking the exit and heading to Nava's.

***

Silvia leaned forward in her queen-size tub to allow her husband to sit behind her. He'd already bathed her and now he wanted to massage her temples and shoulders. She leaned back into him. "Ohh, that feels so good," she told him, the moment he squeezed her neck and shoulders.

"You like that?" KP titled her head, pulled her hair aside and began sucking her neck.

"Ooooooh, yes."

He then reached around and palmed her breasts. He gently pinched her nipples.

Silvia had been so pent-up that she laughed and farted at the same time. She felt embarrassed. "Oh," she jumped and when seeing the bubbles around them, she stood.

"No, no, no. Silvia. Where you going?"

"I'm getting out of this tub, KP. I—I can't believe I just did that."

"You tripping. Hell, I've farted in the tub plenty of times, babe." He pulled her back down onto him and said, "Many times, I done stuck my tongue in that motherfucker."

Hearing those words, Silvia thought about Somolia. She asked him, "You want me to clean it out right quick?"

Before she could turn to face her husband, he'd already slid a finger in there and began pumping and twirling it. "Let me do it."

Silvia positioned herself to where she was on all fours and KP was sitting behind her. She could feel the hot water enter her and more than anything, she could feel herself inviting him in, pleading for him to enter her with something other than his finger. Tonight, she was going to follow Somolia's instructions to the tee.

***

Somolia stepped out of her shower, wrapped a huge beach towel around herself and made her way to the door. It was only one person expected at this hour and she'd been waiting for him ever since she left work. "I'm coming," she whispered to herself before swinging the door open. "Um, can I help you?"

Buddy smiled down at her and nodded. "I sure hope so." He let himself in and closed the door behind him.

"Stop, Buddy. You're hurting me." Somolia pushed at him to no avail and seeing her strength couldn't move him, she palmed his erection with both hands and told him, "I'll pull this motherfucker off, nigga."

Buddy slid a finger between her legs, coating it with her juices.

"Damn!" Somolia's eyes followed his hand, she saw how wet she'd become. She squeezed him harder, toyed with his zipper until she freed his thick dick and with the head of it, she massaged between her huge breasts. "You gonna make me hurt you."

Buddy leaned down, grabbed Somolia under each ass cheek and easily lifted her. He bounced her until she reached back and placed the head of him at her wet vagina. He pushed into her until he was balls' deep.

"Ssss," Somolia inhaled through her teeth, feeling all of him, every wall-stretching inch of his thickness. She wrapped her arms around his neck and held on. By the time he did lower her, they'd made it to her den and he was laying her on the plush carpeting. Buddy positioned her on her back and once he pushed both her thighs to the sides of her breasts, he watched himself enter her repeatedly. He watched his cum-streaked dick disappear over and over and when he was sure he was good and wet, he pushed his dick in her ass.

Somolia's eyes rolled and her body quaked more times than she could count and as soon as she felt Buddy swell inside of her, she told him, "It's yours, babe. It's yours. Fuck this ass, babe, fuck it."

CHAPTER SIX

Thirty minutes later, King was standing in front of Nava's door. He checked both her patio area and the parking area for any sign that a group of unruly guys could have left. There were no beer cans, no cigarette butts or anything else to show what could have been a small gathering—like the one Nava described. He knocked on her door three times.

"King?"

"Yeah, it's me, Nava."

Nava swung the door open and jumped into his arms. "Oh, King, I was so scared."

"Are you all right?"

"I am now. I'm glad you could come."

King walked past a smiling Nava, still not believing that she'd make up something so fictitious just to keep him from spending time with Diamond.

Nava stepped aside, allowing King entry. She was hoping the oversized kitten t-shirt, and tight lace boy shorts appealed to him. She'd planned this very moment just right. Right before she was able to close the door behind him, Diamond stepped inside.

"Hey, Nava. Are you all right?"

Nava's smile immediately faded and was replaced with narrowly-slit eyes and tightened brows. "Uh, excuse me?"

Diamond smiled while walking past her and standing beside King. "I asked if you were all right." She then went on to look around the cramped apartment and its skimpy furnishings. "This is nice, Nava. It fits you perfectly."

Nava rolled her eyes and walked to where she was standing in front of her ex-fiancé. "Thanks for coming, King. I knew I could count on you."

"Why didn't you just call security, Nava? You do have that available to you."

"Because I didn't want to involve the security for just a hunch."

"But, you'd rather call me while I'm clear across town?" King watched her with a disapproving expression.

"I, I'm sorry, King. I wasn't thinking, I guess." Nava hugged him, looked up into his eyes and told him, "I needed you here."

"That is so sweet," Diamond told them in a sing-song voice. "That reminds me of me and my brother at times."

King stepped away from Nava and told her, "Well, it looks as if you're good now." He reached for Diamond and pulled her to him. "Just call security the next time, Nava. That's what the lease includes." He turned Diamond towards the door and followed her out, leaving Nava standing in the center of her living room wearing the net and hook she thought would hold King there.

Nava slowly closed her door and watched them from her bay window as they made their way to the car. She looked back at the candles she'd lit, the bottle of wine on ice, and the warm honey she placed on the towel beside the pallet she laid out for them. "This bitch has got to go," she told herself, seeing King run around and open the door for Diamond. She watched as the two shared kisses, watched as King felt her up and even watched as Diamond looked up at the bay window and waved at her. "Bitch!"

***

Chris helped Datrina close up the salon and once the curlers had cooled off and the dryers were cleaned and unplugged, he took a seat in the swivel chair next to her station. He spun himself to where he could see his girl. He admired her work ethics with the way she organized each station, stocked the shelves and made sure all the chairs faced the same direction. He watched her move about, the way her thighs moved, her hips and ass, finding himself licking his lips when seeing her lips move. He adjusted himself in the chair.

"Why are you sitting over there starting at me like that? Do I need to grab some scissors or something?"

"What?"

"You're over there looking like you're about to put a mask on and take something," she told him, before bending over in front of him.

"If you keep on doing that, I just might." Chris began to stand.

"Chris, stop it." Datrina smiled, looked around them and said, "The lights are still on and the blinds are still open and I don't have time to be hunting down anybody for putting us up on some social media site."

"Well, you need to hurry up so we can go home where the lights are off and the blinds stay closed." He walked up behind her and kissed her neck.

"So, what are we going to do, Chris?" she asked, getting serious. There had been topics around the salon lately and she wanted to know where they stood in their relationship.

"About what?" He kissed her again, turned her so they faced each other and kissed her lips. "Chocolate ass."

"I'm talking about us, Chris. What are we going to do? Are we going to keep being this Bonnie and Clyde couple, or are we going to settle down and start our own family?"

Chris walked her over to the swivel chair and pulled her down into his lap.

"What?"

"Are you pregnant, Datrina?"

"Nigga, you ain't been putting in work like that," she laughed. "You know I'm still on the pills."

Chris looked up in thought. That was something he hadn't been thinking about, them raising a family of their own. "You sure you want to raise a family in this lifestyle?"

"In mine or yours?"

"Both. I mean, your lifestyle is mine and mine is yours."

"Well, now that Silvia is stepping back, maybe we should do the same. We've been blessed to have survived as long as we have, Chris. We've made enough money to support a couple of families, gotten away with things we shouldn't have and been there for each other through whatever." Datrina positioned herself where she could see his eyes. "Why keep pushing it, babe?"

"Life has a way of trapping you, babe, and you're right.We have been fortunate." Chris exhaled. "You know I got at Dell about finding us a house, don't you?"

Datrina sat up and smiled. "Oh yeah?"

"Yep." Chris nodded slowly, while rocking her in his lap.

"You're serious, aren't you?"

"We should be looking at something real nice real soon." He reached for her hand and kissed it.

"I've heard this before, Chris. Has Diamond seen it?"

"Nope, but she was the one that insisted Dell get the ball rolling and that half a million wasn't enough."

Datrina stood. "Half a million ain't enough?"

"You know how Diamond is when it comes to you."

"Oh my God! What kind of house does she want us to have, Chris?"

"I told you, something real nice." Chris laughed and pulled her back onto him and smiled.

"You're one sick puppy, Chris."

"Speaking of sick puppy, I think I walked in on Diamond masturbating this morning."

"Again?"

"Yep, and she was watching that movie *Tammy* again. That's sick."

Datrina punched him. "Shut up, Chris. That girl wasn't masturbating to no damn comedy."

"Hmmph."

"Wait until I tell Diamond."

Chris laughed at the memory. "You should have seen her. She looked back at me smiling like she was crazy. I knew she was doing something, but I just snatched the remote and made her ass get up."

"You be hatin', Chris."

"Whatever."

"Well, hopefully, King's taking care of her now."

Those words filled Chris' mind and thinking of just that, he pushed Datrina. "Well, let's get you home, so I can take care of you."

***

After their bath and Silvia's anal cleaning, KP followed his wife to the bedroom they shared. He caressed her gently, massaged her from head to toe, and just as he was about to enter her, she stopped him. "Wait a minute, KP."

"What's wrong?" KP lay there with the hardest erection he'd had in a long time. He watched his wife.

"I don't want you to make love to me. I want to be fucked. Hard." Silvia thought about some of the things she'd heard in the salon, and average and mediocre wasn't going to do it anymore. KP's flaw was that he always wanted to make love. He was always lovey-dovey and Silvia wanted spontaneity. She wanted to feel dominated every once in a while.

"Um, okay. I'm cool with that."

Silvia remained standing, wanting to see just how much of it he understood and seeing him with no clue of what he was to do, she folded her arms and waited.

"I mean, what you do want me to do, babe?" KP shrugged in confusion.

Silvia sighed, closed her eyes and spit it out. "Take the pussy, KP. Make me feel as if you're taking what's yours—what belongs to you."

KP frowned, eased to the edge of the bed and contemplated his next move. This was the first time she'd requested such and it confused him. Where he always thought he was pleasing her sexually, it was now making sense. The many times she stepped out on him wasn't because she didn't love him, it was because he wasn't satisfying her in this setting. KP swallowed, stood and eased up to his wife.

Silvia switched her stance and looked up at him with question, watched him as he watched her. Finally, she shook her head and sighed. "Don't even worry about it, Kevin." She walked past him, went into the bathroom and locked the door. Her mind raced as she thought about the talk she had with a Q a short time ago. She even thought about the many times Somolia gave detailed descriptions of the ways her man fucked her. They never made love, only fucked and at this time in her life, Silvia wanted just that.

KP watched as his wife locked herself in the bathroom. He thought about the many times he'd talked to Q about sex and the difference in their outlook on the subject. Where KP felt making love was the right way to sex his wife, Q was always the one to express the fact that women loved to be fucked down. They liked to be dominated, submissive with their men even. And, to hear his wife voice that same perception, he couldn't help but think that they'd gone behind his back to find such adventure, such spontaneous actions. The picture of his best friend and his wife filled his thoughts and before he knew it, he was half-dressed. At first, he started to charge Silvia up about the things he was thinking but thought better of it, after remembering the little talk he and Chris had. All he knew was that Q had to go and he didn't have a year to wait for Chris to settle his issues.

The following morning

Diamond was awakened by the sounds of running water and Beyonce's hit, "Lemonade." She rolled over. Immediately registering the fact that she wasn't in her room or any room in the McClendon mansion, she looked herself over. She wore sheer panties and bra and was wrapped in satin sheets. It took four seconds to remember that once they made it back to King's apartment, they had a few drinks, talked and . . .

"Good morning, beautiful." King stood in the doorway in only his silk pajama pants. His chest bare—chiseled, abs packed up and his shoulders broad.

Diamond swallowed. "I thought we were going to get a room last night?"

"We were, but it had gotten late and—"

"Or, did you get me drunk, drop me off and go back to your wife?" Diamond knew better, but still found a way to say the first thing that came to mind.

King smiled, walked over to where she lay and kissed her. "I've been watching you sleep for most of the morning."

"Really?"

"Yep. I saw you stirring and went to start a shower."

Diamond sat up, noticed her clothes were neatly folded and sitting in the chair by the bedroom window. "You undressed me, King?"

"Do you remember anything?"

"Vaguely."

King laughed. "Let's just say you don't ever need to drink again, Diamond. You lost control and did some things I'm sure you wouldn't have if—"

"What did I do, King? Go ahead and tickle your fantasy."

"You blew my mind. You damn near raped me."

Nigga, please. If anything, you sat over there and jacked off on me while I was sleep." She looked down at his crotch, saw a slight bulge and tsked.

"Is that what you think?"

"Ain't no telling." She watched him move towards her, his bulge shifting as he did.

"Well, sorry to disappoint you, but I have a little something better in mind."

"And what would that be?"

King yanked the satin sheets from over her and began pulling at her panties. He wrestled her until she finally gave in. He undid her bra, freeing her palm-sized breasts. "Let's go shower right quick."

"So, now I stink." Diamond scooted to the edge of the bed.

"I didn't say that, Diamond."

"You're showing it, King."

He pushed her back onto the bed and parted her legs and before she could raise any protest, he licked her clit twice, pulled on her pussy lips and stuck his tongue inches inside her now wet, moist walls.

She moaned. "Nigga, you've got to do more than that now," she told him while parting her legs even more. Diamond watched him work her with his tongue, encouraged him with her moans and invited him to more when she reached down and parted her lips for him.

"You're a freak, Diamond," he mumbled between slurps and licks. King stood, stepped out of his pants and grabbed his now erect penis at its base. He watched her turn on her side and raise her leg for him. She fingered herself while he watched and once her juices coated her fingers, she stuck them in her mouth. She was no stranger at pleasing herself and was challenging him to do better. Hoping he could.

King kissed her stomach, licked her breasts, her neck and found her lips. With both skill and precision, he slid his tongue into her mouth and his dick into her sex simultaneously. He frowned at how tight she was. He was about to stop until she began pulling him in deeper, all the while looking into his eyes.

***

Somolia rolled over and reached for Buddy. They'd done their thing the night before and she really wanted to stay in and spend time with him. She looked towards her bathroom. "Buddy?" It wasn't until she stood and looked over at the dresser that she noticed the fold-out card beside ten, crisp hundred-dollar-bills. She sighed before picking up the card and reading.

To a wonderful woman and a wonderful night, till next time.

Buddy.

She ran her fingers over the bills and smiled. As much as she liked the way he spoiled her, she still wanted to spend time with him. She wanted to know more about her man. With all that was going on and her salon about to open, she wanted to at least tell him of her good fortune. As she walked from her bedroom to her kitchen for a glass of water, the doorbell startled her. She smiled while making her way to the door. "Buddy, I'm coming." She laughed when hearing the words aloud because she'd been doing a lot of that lately. She swung the door open.

"Hey, babe."

"Q?" Somolia frowned and after realizing she'd answered the door naked, tried to hide behind it.

"I was in the area and thought I'd stop by. I didn't see any car out front and said fuck it." Q smiled, winked and let himself in.

"I'm not dressed, Q. I—"

"You acting like I haven't seen you naked before." Q walked past her and made his way towards her kitchen, subtly looking for any signs of her having company.

"Q, can you please wait outside?" Somolia looked towards the street, praying Buddy didn't step out only to return shortly.

"Why?" Q did his search and walked up to Somolia. It was evident he'd been drinking and by the way he was acting, it was recently done at that.

Somolia closed her eyes and raised her hand in front of her. "Q, leave."

"Oh, I can't come by anymore?" he asked while backing her against her living room wall.

"You're drunk, Q."

"I'm drunk?" Q reached for one of her breasts. "Ain't it better when I'm like this?"

"Q, stop! Just stop."

"A nigga can't get his dick sucked no more. You got a man now and I can't stop by and get my shit sucked no more?" He pressed her against the wall, bent down and tried to rub between her legs. "This pussy ain't mine anymore, Somolia?"

"No, it's not. Now will you please get out before he comes back?" Somolia tried to grab his wrist and keep him from touching her, from feeling how wet she still was.

"Just let me taste it and I'll leave, Somolia. I promise. I just want to taste it."

Somolia sighed, hoping he'd stay true to his word. She placed his hand between her legs and then, pushed his fingers into his mouth.

"Umm," he moaned with closed eyes.

"Will you leave now?"

"You can't do me like that, Somolia. Let me taste it myself. Please." Q pulled her to him, reached down and kissed her lips. "I've missed you, babe."

"I'm with somebody else now, Q. I'm—"

Q stuck his tongue in her mouth and forcefully pulled her unto the couch. He held her down with one hand and undid his pants with the other.

She knew her strength was no match for his and instead of fighting with him, she relented. Experience taught her that when they really wanted it, they'd get it. She told him, "Hurry up, Q, damn."

"Turn over, right quick. Turn over."

"Just hurry up, Q."

"You know I love you, don't you?" He fumbled with his pants until his dick spilled out.

"Yeah, whatever."

"I'm serious, Somolia. You're my girl." He pushed himself into her wetness, slapped her ass until she raised it and once she was face down and ass up, he banged her roughly. "This is my pussy," he told her, before grabbing her by the neck. He continued to pump her vigorously while slightly choking her. Something she'd come to love. Something that made her cum harder than she normally would.

Somolia reached back, spread her cheeks and pushed back into him. She knew how to make Q cum and the faster he did, the sooner he'd leave. Feeling him swell, she told him, "Fuck my ass, Q. Fuck me in my ass, babe."

Q slid into her without missing a stroke. He pushed her face into the couch, fucked her hard and deep and when he came, he collapsed onto her. "I'll kill a nigga behind you, Somolia. You hear me? I'll kill a nigga behind this ass."

"Yeah, I feel you and you need to get your trifling ass out before that just be the case." Somolia climbed from under him, grabbed his arm and pulled him in the direction of her front door. The sex was good, but Q definitely had to go.

After seeing Q out and closing her door, Somolia put her back to it and closed her eyes. She'd taught Q everything she liked, loved and expected when it came to sex, but now that she'd found bigger and better and a man just as eager to learn her as Q had, she wasn't going to mess that up. And, after what just happened, she prayed things wouldn't get fucked up.

Nicole Goosby

CHAPTER SEVEN

Nava walked out her front door, thinking of a lie to tell so King would come see her. The things she had planned for the two of them the night before was still fresh on her mind and she was sure that if only she could get him away from Diamond, they would rekindle their relationship and she'd be that much closer to her primary agenda. She dialed his number a second time and after being sent to voicemail, she immediately called back. Being so early in the morning, there was only one place he could be and thinking of just that, visions of him with Diamond filled her thoughts. She remembered the ways they sexed each other, the ways she did him and the many things he did to her. She cut several lines on the small saucer she carried and snorted the entire line with the ten-dollar bill she'd rolled earlier.

"Fuck you, Diamond!" Nava said, thinking out loud. "Nobody takes what's rightfully mine. King's dick is mine to the core!" She walked back inside and slammed the door, slid the saucer on the dining table, grabbed a mango-hazed filled blunt and fired it up. She had to get high. This was the only way she could get her head right, and this was the only way she'd be able to rid herself of the thoughts Diamond gave her.

***

After leaving King's apartment, Diamond made her way to Datrina and Chris's spot. It was still early and she was sure they were both there. She parked, jumped out of her Corvette and made her way inside.

Diamond used her key to enter. "Datrina! Chris!" she called out while making her way to their bedroom. It would be right up her alley to catch both of them under covers. "Chris!"

"Diamond, why the hell you running through here yelling like crazy?"

Chris met her before she could make it down the hall of their loft.

"Where's Datrina?" Diamond smiled at him.

"She went to work. Why?" Chris walked past her, moved towards his kitchen area.

"We got to talk," she told him while placing her phone on the counter and jumping unto the stool before her.

"What about, Diamond?" Chris handed her an ice tea, grabbed himself a juice and faced her. He frowned.

Diamond continued to smile.

"And you got the same shit on from yesterday," he told her with a look of disgust.

"I gave him some pussy this morning." Diamond closed her eyes and bit her bottom lip, as if adding emphasis.

Chris snatched the bottle he'd just given her. "You did what?"

"I fucked King, nigga. I put this pussy on him."

"You a nasty bitch, Diamond."

She snatched the bottle back from him. "Jealous-ass nigga."

"Ain't nobody jealous of your nasty ass. You don't even know that nigga like that and you laying up with him." Chris walked from the kitchen to his den. He placed himself on the suede sectional, shook his head and turned up the juice he held.

"Well, I know him enough to know that he can fuck. That nigga fucked me with my legs closed, Chris." She made her eyes roll upward before telling him, "I thought I was going to die. That nigga's dick so big—"

"I don't want to hear about that nigga's dick. You're sick." Chris turned his lips up to her.

"I came like four times back-to-back, nigga, and then he ate my pussy until I came again."

Chris sighed, shook his head and laughed. He knew what she was doing and since they were on the subject, he was going to give her a little game. "Did he stick his tongue in your ass?"

"Yep."

"Did he push your legs to your breasts and let you see that motherfucker stretching your shit?" Before she could respond to his question, he went on. "He opened that ass up and spit in it? He bit them nipples? He made you suck his dick when changing positions, huh? He spanked that ass until you came? He—"

"Shut your punk ass up, nigga. He didn't do all that shit." Diamond frowned.

Satisfied with what he was and wasn't hearing, Chris leaned back. "Then, he ain't did shit. If that nigga ain't run over your skinny ass, slide you across some carpet and slap you with the dick, he ain't did shit to remember."

She defended King's lack of sexual abuse upon her. "That was just the first time, nigga, damn."

"Hell, a nigga's supposed to break a bitch off every time. Gangsters ain't got time to play with no pussy. Humph!"

"Well, whatever. It felt good to me and that's all that matters." Diamond leaned toward the arm of the couch and closed her eyes.

Chris watched her, took a swig of his juice and told her, "It's about time, Diamond."

"About time for what?"

"That someone made you feel like a woman—showed you something other than that tomboy shit you be on at times."

"Nigga, I know I'm a woman. You acting like I just found out I had pussy or something. I know what's between my legs."

"Well, you could have fooled me. The way you be looking at my girl and shit be having a nigga second guessing you at times." Chris laughed.

Diamond reached behind her and threw a pillow towards him. "She's lucky I'm not bi-sexual. I would have been tasting her black ass."

"See what I'm talking about?" Chris shook his head, thinking about all the times they went shopping, did lunch together and hung out at the mansion. He smiled at the visual. "I'm happy for you though, Diamond. You're not one of these hoes running around here fucking every nigga that claim he's got something to give."

"You know better than that. I keep my pussy tight for a reason."

"Just be careful with that shit because when you start fucking a nigga, you attach yourself emotionally and sometimes spiritually and when they fuck over you, it hurt."

"Hopefully I won't have to worry about that."

Chris nodded. "Hopefully not. Because if he does, I'm going to kill him, Diamond. So, make sure he understands that it's non-negotiable."

She opened her eyes, looked over at Chris and looked off. She knew his words were gold. She also knew that if King did mess over her, she'd most likely encourage Chris to do so.

***

KP stopped himself from leaving. He thought about where things were going with his wife and wasn't about to let her slip away again. He hated thinking she'd done such things, but he now knew the reasons she would. He walked back towards their bedroom, checked the knob on the bathroom door and told his wife, "Open this door, Silvia."

"I'm busy, Kevin."

"Do I have to break this door, Silvia?"

"What do you want?"

"Open this door."

He could hear her mumble under her breath, the toilet flushing and the sink water being run. He stood there.

"What, Kevin?" Silvia opened the door and stepped out.

KP grabbed her arm and pulled her towards the bed. "You want to be fucked, huh?"

"K—"

KP pushed her onto the bed and climbed onto it behind her. He spanked her ass cheeks.

Kevin, Stop it."

He wrestled her down until she was flat on her back and reached over to grab the t-shirt beside them on the floor. He tied her hands above her head, bit her neck and told her, "Open your legs." He then began rubbing her clit violently.

He cut her off by biting her neck harder. "Open your legs wider."

"They are. They can't open any farther than that, boy." She shifted under him.

With no hands, KP found the entrance of her vagina and pushed deep inside of her. He felt her suck air through her teeth. "Damn, this pussy's tight," he told her before pumping her slowly. He freed her hands so he could raise her leg, allowing him to go deeper.

Silvia bit her husband's lip, grabbed him around his neck and choked him as hard as she could until he wrestled her hands from around him.

"This is my pussy!" he yelled, after pulling his lip from her mouth. "This is my shit." Kevin held his wife's leg with one hand and balanced himself with the other. He watched himself stroke her. He watched as her pussy grip his erection and when thinking that his best friend had done the same, he began fucking her harder, faster. "This is how you want it, huh? This is what you want?"

Silvia threw her hips at him, matching him stroke for stroke and the harder he gave it to her, the harder she threw it back at him. She yelped every time he hit the bottom of her, moaned every time he angled a stroke. This was definitely what she wanted. "Is that all you got, nigga? Is that as hard as you can fuck it?"

When feeling his wife raise both of her legs, KP planted both his fists on each side of her head, spread his legs and fucked her faster, deeper and harder, the sounds of their flesh rhythmically slapping, her moans matching each of his grunts. He closed his eyes tight and while envisioning different men sex his wife, he knew he had to be better, had to go harder and this is what he'd have to do from now on. "This is my pussy, babe. Tell me it's mine."

***

Nava checked her phone to make sure she hadn't missed calls from King. She'd already talked to her connect and ordered another ounce of the work she'd been getting and she was horny. She hadn't had sex in a couple of days and wanted to feel King inside of her again. She phoned him.

***

King was pulling sheets from the dryer when his phone rang. He and Diamond had wet his sheets so much, he had to wash them. He knew he didn't do some of the things he should have and was really hoping she wouldn't hold it against him or think he was just a lame in the bed. King knew he had more in him and swore the next time, would be the one she remembered.

Seeing Nava's picture on his phone, he sighed before answering. "What's up, Nava?"

"Hey, babe. Where've you been? I've been calling you all morning?"

"Diamond spent the night and we woke up a little later than expected." King knew mentioning Diamond would take the seduction out of the tone she was using.

"Um, I take it she's gone now."

"Yep, she had some things she needed to do."

"Oh, she got the dick and left, huh?"

"Nava, what do you want?"

"I want to talk to you about what we started the last time," she pouted.

King exhaled and told her, "I am not buying you a strip club, Nava. That's something we're not going to talk about again."

"Well, just come over here so we can come to some kind of agreement, because I don't want to talk business over this phone. You know someone's always listening to these things."

King laughed. Her methods were so obvious.

"Besides, I made this banana pudding for you and I'm about to order some pizza."

"Pizza?"

"Yep, you remember how we used to lay up and run through boxes of Domino's Pizza?"

"How can I forget, Nava?"

"Remember that time?"

King's mind drifted to all the good times he shared with his ex. He thought about the promises they made, the wedding she planned and the honeymoon they were going to enjoy. King found himself missing the woman he used to know and love.

"You hear me, King?"

"Yeah, I'm listening to you."

"What happened to us? I mean, I know I left for a little while, but for you to be so in with that bitch makes me question all we had. You just met her, King—how can you love her after only a couple of months?"

"I've known her longer than that, Nava." He thought about how Diamond came into his life. He thought about the lies, the secrets and the love it brought. He told her, "We've been through more than you'll ever know."

"You still have feelings for me, King?"

"Yeah, how can I not?"

"Do you really have feelings for me, King?"

King nodded. "Yes, Nava. I do. I really do."

"Then show me, Kengyon Johnson. Come make love to me."

"Nava, you tripping."

"Please."

"No, I'm not going to do Diamond like that. You wouldn't want me to do you like that. Would you?"

"Please, King. Please. Just this one time."

"Nava, stop asking me because I'm going to keep saying no."

"Well, just come over here and watch me fuck myself, like you used to."

"I have some—"

"If you've ever loved me, King—if it was never a lie, you'll come."

King relented. He wasn't about to continue to go back and forth with her over something they both knew to be true, something that was real at one time. "Give me about an hour, Nava. I'll try to stop by there."

"Thanks, babe."

"Whatever, Nava."

"I love you and I'll see you in a hour."

Nava threw her phone on the sectional King bought for her, flipped through her playlist until she found some old-school SWV and turned up the volume. She was definitely going to show King what he was missing. And, to get herself right, she dipped her finger into the baggie she had, covered its tip with the powdery substance and massaged her clit. Hoping this time spent with King would be something he lied to Diamond about, she positioned her phone to where she could record the whole thing. This would be the setting that ran his new girlfriend off. Nava smiled, emptied the remaining powder on the saucer and rolled a fresh ten-dollar-bill.

***

Camille was sitting on the passenger's side of Buddy's Dually looking over a few texts. King had called to tell her he'd be at her place once they returned and she returned one to Diamond, telling her she'd go with her to visit Antonio the upcoming weekend. She and Buddy made the trip to Houston and were awaiting a call from one of her buyers. Now that they had a few minutes together, she had a ton of questions for him. "You and this Somolia woman seem to be getting serious." She glanced over at him and completed her text.

"You can say that," he told her in his deep vocal.

"You know how women are, Buddy. When we find new toys, we use them up until better comes along."

"So do men."

"I see the effort she's making with you, so I can't necessarily say she's using you, but I just need you to be careful."

"She's a good woman, Boss Lady, and I'm really wanting to see where this is headed. At first, I thought it was just going to be a sex thing, but it's turned into something more."

"So, she's sexing you better than you have been?" Camille looked over at her friend and smiled.

"Much better. She's the freakiest woman I've ever met in my life."

"Really?" Camille turned herself to where she could face him. She needed to hear more and she needed to gauge his reactions.

Buddy nodded. "She's a motherfucker too."

"That little fat chick at the salon?" she asked, unable to visualize Somolia in that light.

"Are you pleasing her?"

"As far as I can tell."

"What does her body tell you? That's the sign that tells you what you're doing right and what you're doing wrong."

Buddy thought about all the times Somolia's body convulsed, all the times they had to place towels under her so she wouldn't soak the sheets as much, or leave wet spots on the carpets. He nodded again. "Yeah, I'm definitely doing that."

"Does she talk to you while you're fucking her?'

"All the time."

"She makes you feel as if you're the only man and dick in the world?"

"She makes me feel as if I'm the king of her castle. She—"

"She's training you, Buddy, and at the same time investing in it. You have to be careful with her. She knows what she's doing." Camille's thoughts went to Nava and all the other women like her. She told him, "Make her show you trust, watch how she lies to other people and you'll always know when she's lying to you."

"Yes, ma'am."

"And, if I ever find out that you can't see past her bullshit, I'm going to boil her fat ass. We're going to put some potatoes around her ass, pour some gravy on her, bust down a loaf of bread and unfold a couple of napkins."

Buddy laughed. "As long as I get the ass."
Camille laughed. "Um, that might be the best part of it."
"It is. Believe me, it is."

CHAPTER EIGHT

After his conversation with Nava and a text to Camille, King phoned Diamond. He couldn't get her off his mind and more than anything, he wanted her to know that there was much more in store for her. That morning she'd surprised the hell out of him and just thinking about it caused him to smile continually.

"Hello?"

Hearing the male voice, King checked to make sure he'd called the correct number. "Um, hello?"

"Yeah, what's up?'

"Chris?" he asked, knowing there was only one male she was known to have in her company.

"Is this King?"

"Yeah, yeah—is Diamond around?" King sighed, that same smile finding him again.

"Yeah, she's in the shower at the moment. What's up?"

"Aw, nothing. I was just calling to see what she was doing and to tell her that I was about to run by Nava's right quick."

"Oh, yeah?"

"Yeah, you know how it goes." King knew how much Diamond meant to Chris and therefore wasn't tripping when the questions began.

"So, y'all fucking now?"

King laughed. "Is that what she told you?'

"Yeah, she said something about you not knowing what to do with it or something like that. I overheard her and my girl talking earlier," Chris lied.

"She said that?"

"I might have heard her wrong, but if not, you need to step your game up."

"Yeah, yeah. Definitely."

"Diamond's a good woman but she's a freak, King, and you have to tie a bitch like her up, I mean—"

"I know exactly what you mean, Chris."

"And, she has to know she's the only one. Don't fuck this up, King, because I'd hate for this shit to become personal between me and you."

"You have my word, Chris. You got that." King understood.

"Well, I'll make sure she gets back at you when she's finished."

King lowered his phone and smiled. He told himself, "I can't believe she said that." Either way, he was going to blow her mind the next go-around. And, he was going to show her just how much she meant to him. Remembering his promise to Nava, he grabbed his keys and headed out.

***

Raymond's arrival was unexpected and that was the way he wanted it. He parked alongside Dell's Bentley and climbed out. There were a few things he wanted to see for himself and with several other stops to make, he took the stairs two at a time.

Dell made his way to the door, ready to curse the person that continually rang his doorbell. His last couple of weeks hadn't gone as planned and it seemed there was no favor in sight. He looked out of his opaque window sidings, saw the lone figure standing out there and opened the door. "Raymond, what the hell you doing here this early?"

Raymond pushed past him. "*Early* is four- or five-thirty in the morning. Your ass should have been up."

"Well, come on in," Dell told him, while groggily wiping sleep from his eyes and following Raymond into the kitchen.

"What do you have for drinking in this motherfucker?" Raymond opened the stainless steel refrigerator door and pulled out a beer. He handed another to Dell.

"You're in a good mood this morning," Dell told him before popping the top.

"I'm doing the books and I need to see the money, get an accurate account of what's going and coming."

"Um, I have the paperwork filed and the USB drive I gave you has everything that matters."

"Yeah, that's cool, but I need to see the money. We need to do a hard count."

"A hard count for what?" Dell frowned.

Raymond knew this would be the play Dell used to begin an argument to the fact and he was prepared. "Didn't Antonio call you already? He wants to see where we at—said he's about to make a move and needs to assure his step or something."

Dell thought about the fact that he could have missed Antonio's call for not wanting to be bothered. "He might have, but—"

"Well, let's get to it, because he has me doing other things for him today." Raymond stood beside the grand piano Dell prided himself in and smiled. It was finally time for the truth.

"Man, I'm not about to count all this money," Dell told him before making his way to the mini bar.

"That's why I'm here."

Dell swallowed the dark liquor. "Aahhh."

"Come on, nigga. I've got shit to do."

Dell walked over, unlatched the locks around the piano and once they were looking at millions of dollars in hundred-dollar-bills, he stepped back.

"Where's the other location?"

"The same place it's always been—in the safety deposit boxes."

"Get the keys, because we're going there next." Raymond began pulling out the stacks of bills before them. He was no stranger of money and knew there had to be more. Much more.

Dell stood and watched him. There was no way he was going to count all the money he had there, let alone want to go to the bank and count what was said to be in that location. He began helping his friend. His phone rang. That had to be Antonio.

"Hey."

"What's up, Dell?"

"Chris?" Dell questioned the voice on the other end of his line. "What happened, man?"

"Some shit came up and it had to be taken care of."

"You should have called or something, man. I had to take—" Dell stopped himself after seeing Raymond busy himself with the money. He hadn't told Raymond about the money he'd taken out to pay off some of the guys he dealt with, because he was hoping Chris came through on his end.

"I called you a couple of times this morning, but didn't leave any message on your voicemail."

"So, what's up?" Dell walked to where he could conduct his call with Chris in private.

"I was hoping I could look at the property today."

"Um, I'm in the middle of something right now and I don't know how long this is going to take. You should have got at me before now."

"I—" Chris was cut off.

Dell didn't realize Diamond had snatched the phone from Chris at the other end of the line until he heard her call his name.

"Dell?"

Dell closed his eyes before answering, "Diamond."

"I need to see the property I inquired about. We're trying to make moves and we need to take care of this right away."

"I'm still yet to—"

"I'm not trying to hear that shit, nigga. If you had some work for a bitch to move, you would have been burring a bitch phone up. Me and Chris driving out to Irving and you need to be there with that half a million we talked about."

"Diamond, I haven't even got in touch with the realtors."

"I have, and they're meeting us at the property today and I'm not going to show us half-stepping. I told Antonio what was up and he told me to tell you to make it happen."

"That property was well over one million dollars, Diamond, and—"

"We're paying cash and I'm more than sure them hoes going to dance when the music starts."

"Give me a couple of hours to get the money together. I'll be there," he reluctantly agreed. The half a million was the least of his concerns and when thinking of the words he'd told Raymond a day prior, it was a growing one.

"Oh yeah. Antonio wants us to move all the money from your house. He says it's an unnecessary risk."

"He said what?" Dell had to have heard her speak of something else.

"Wrap that shit up, nigga. We moving the money. Too many people know where you live and motherfuckers been talking."

Dell held his tongue. He wanted to tell her she brought KP to his home. He wanted to tell her he was more than sure she had something to do with the decisions her brother made regarding him and the way he'd been doing things for the longest.

"And where are we moving it to?"

"He hasn't told me yet. Just get it ready because after we buy that property in Irving, we're moving it. All of it."

Dell could feel the blood pumping through his forehead. She always had to be the one to add insult to injury, butane to an already lit flame and tons of extra weight to his already overwhelmed shoulders. He'd warned Raymond about Diamond many times before, and it was obvious he still wasn't seeing it. "Diamond says Antonio wants to move the money. Said something about too many people knowing where I stay."

Raymond stood and nodded. "He has a very valid point."

"Can't you see what that bitch is doing, nigga?"

"Who? Diamond?"

"Yeah, Diamond. The bitch taking over, Raymond. I told you about this."

"Motherfucker, Antonio must have made the call."

Dell walked over to where he stood and brought his fist down hard on the piano. "She had something to do with it. I'm willing to bet you, nigga."

"You tripping. Either way, it's his money. If the nigga want to donate this shit, that's on him. Why does it matter that she's the one delivering the message?"

"Did you know that she and Chris are about to buy a one-million-dollar home today?"

"That's it?"

"Yeah, motherfucker and we putting up half of it."

Raymond tsked. "That ain't shit. Hell, my house costs more than that and if Chris is matching the money we putting up, that's even better. It's about time he and Datrina found themselves something nice."

There was no reasoning with Raymond. There never was when it came to the things he couldn't see.

"Well," Raymond pointed to the stacks and bundles before them, "that's half a million right there. You take that and head out to meet them and I'll finish with the counts. After I'm done here, I'll then stop by the bank to get that money also." Raymond shrugged and held out his hand.

"What's that for?"

"The safety deposit keys, nigga. Where they at?"

***

Camille and Buddy were pulling in just as King was stepping out of her studio. Seeing the both of them in good spirits put both a smile on his face and a thought in his head. He wanted all of them to put a dinner together. He wanted to see the family they were becoming. "I have an idea," he told the two of them as they neared him.

"And, what would that be, King?" Camille stopped in front of him, looked him over and glanced in Buddy's direction.

"What?" King asked, seeing her actions.

"We're waiting to hear of this grand idea you have, aren't we, Buddy?"

"Yes, ma'am."

"Anyway, I was thinking about putting a dinner together." King smiled warmly before placing his hands in his pockets.

"Haven't we done that before?" Camille asked, remembering the dinner they fucked her out of.

"I'm talking about everybody, Camille. Our people, Diamond's people, and Nava."

Camille rolled her eyes and rolled her head. She looked up to see Buddy looking down at her with raised brows, as if the idea was something to approve.

"Pussy got y'all feeling like that?" She walked off, leaving the both of them standing there. "I might need to find me a bitch to fuck if it's that damn good."

King and Buddy looked at each other and smiled. King told him, "I'm about to make a run right quick." He patted Buddy's arm. "Go talk to her."

***

Silvia closed the door behind her husband, walked back into their bedroom and fell across their bed. She exhaled fully. "Shit!" she yelled with closed eyes. *That was definitely worth the wait,* she thought. Whatever had gotten into her husband was something she was hoping would stay. She wanted to call her friend, Datrina, but knew their conversation would eventually be topic of the entire salon. She had to tell someone. She'd called the only other person she could think of at the moment.

"Hey, Silvia. What's up?" Raymond asked, while placing bundles of bills into the suitcases.

"You wouldn't believe what KP just did to me."

"Not again, Silvia. I know he didn't put his hands on you again?"

"His hands, his tongue, his dick and everything else he could grab."

"Silvia."

"Something has gotten into him because he just got through fucking the shit out of me, Raymond. I'm telling you."

"Do you really think I want to hear this right now?"

Silvia rolled over onto her back and smiled at the memory. "Yep."

"Well, I have other things to do besides hear how your husband fucked you last night."

"This morning. I'm talking about just minutes ago."

"It sounds as if you really enjoyed yourself."

"Umm-hmm."

"You're making it sound like the best fuck you ever had."

Silvia laughed. She knew what he was insinuating. She told him, "It's up there, if not."

"Oh really?"

"Really."

"You trying to change that or what?"

Silvia thought better of the things she really wanted to say. She only told him, "If only it had happened with two dicks."

"You're going to talk to him about it?"

"Should I?"

"It's about what you want. Silvia. I'd like to know what he says about it, though."

"Maybe I will. I don't want to push him too fast too soon though."

"The next time I get in that pussy, I'm going to make it mine. You know that, right?"

"The way he worked it, you're going to have to come on with it." Silvia looked towards her bedroom doorway, making sure she was still alone.

"Sounds as if I have something to look forward to."

"We'll see," she told him, before rolling onto her stomach. "Where you at, anyway?"

"I'm at Dell's going over the books."

"Oh yeah, what they look like?" she asked, really regretting it. She'd told all of them that she was stepping back and asking of matters and money that no longer concerned her wasn't something she wanted to start again.

"You know Dell, so you know the money is short."

"Yeah."

"Short as hell at that," he added.

"How short?"

86

"The nigga got a little over three million here."

"Okay, what's wrong with that?"

"Because, the last time I looked over the books, we had over four million at this location."

"Maybe we—maybe y'all need to put the money elsewhere?"

"That's what Antonio's got us doing as we speak."

"Antonio? When did you hear from him? He hasn't called me in a minute."

"Diamond told us."

"Diamond?" Silvia sat upright. This was all new to her.

"Yeah, she said he told her to pick up all the money. Dell went to meet her and Chris at that property in Irving and after that, she's coming to get the rest of it."

"Really?"

"Yep."

"And, you believe her?"

"Why shouldn't I? If her brother wants the money moved, then that's what we're going to do."

Silvia laughed at him. "Well, I'll leave you all to it."

"I'll get at you later, Silvia."

"All right then."

"Oh, yeah, let me know what KP says about that?"

Silvia smiled. "Bye, freak."

***

The sound of Faith Evans' song, "Love Like This Before" filled her living room and a line cut from her new batch filled her nose. Nava danced to the beat that boomed from her stereo system, the high taking her to new heights.

"You sure he's coming?" the guy asked her as he stood.

"He always does," she told him, before spinning herself around and dropping her ass. She'd been dancing for most of her life and knew what men liked to see. She rehearsed her performance in the mirror and now that King was on his way, she showed her supplier first. And seeing the bulge in his jeans, she licked his lips.

"Well, he'd better hurry up before I fuck something." He walked to where she dropped down and fingered her pussy.

She spread her legs more, raised her hips and told him, "When I finish putting this pussy on him, he's going to be begging for me to move back in."

He smelled his fingers before sucking them. "Peach pussy, huh?"

"Kiwi, nigga. Now, get out of here." Nava stood, pushed him towards the door and once he was gone, she put on her oversized sleeping shirt and waited. Tonight, she and her friends were going clubbing and she was in need of a few stacks. After making sure her phone was positioned perfectly, she lit a laced blunt, walked out onto her fenced patio and closed her eyes. It would soon be over and she'd be on her way. But, this time she'd win.

CHAPTER NINE

KP parked at the top of Q's street and waited. He'd made only two stops before finding a guy that was willing to purchase the gun he needed. It took only one hundred dollars for the guy and three hundred dollars for the .38special he palmed while sitting in the cabin of the Escalade Diamond had given him. His mind raced as he waited. He and Q had been friends for over fifteen years and now he wondered how many of those years he'd been going behind his back in pursuit of his wife.

If nothing else, he wanted Q's confession of it. Chris's words blinked in and out of his thoughts, but he couldn't wait. He understood more than anything that Chris wouldn't see or understand the urgency of the situation, because it wasn't his own money that was stolen and it wasn't his wife and best friend that committed such an act.

He understood one thing and KP had to respect it, just as KP was hoping he would also. Despite the threat he was given, he'd have to deal with Chris when that time came, because there was no way he was about to let Q get away with something so personal—twice. Silvia was another story and it was also one he'd have read sooner or later. For now, it wasn't Silvia's fault and it wasn't her problem.

As soon as the sedan pulled past KP, he sighed, thinking it was Q returning. His plans changed continually for not wanting to be suspected in what he was about to do. At first, he thought about walking up on Q as soon as he pulled up—the way Chris did both him and Q under a month ago. But, he decided against it because there were people outside going about their days. Then, he thought about calling Q to some undisclosed location and getting at him, but then he wouldn't be able to get the much-needed confession out of him. And besides, the last thing he needed was for some witness to see what shouldn't have been seen or some cop rolling up on him after hearing a shot or two. That's when he settled on the idea of waiting for Q to arrive at his own home and making it look as if a robbery took place. He'd already had to call the police about a shooting that took place and KP was a witness to that report, so he was hoping this would be looked at as an act that stemmed from it. The reason he selected the revolver was so no shell casing would be found, sent to some forensics lab and checked for prints. As far as he could see, there would be nothing pointing to him once he did get at Q.

He checked his surroundings before climbing out of the truck. Before he went to Q's, he'd make a block and come to the house from a different direction and once he made it to the rear of the house, he'd break in where the air conditioning unit was and wait. He knew where Q kept household items so tape, towels and the like was something he didn't have to purchase.

KP had walked every bit of twenty yards before the Audi pulled alongside him.

"Nigga, where you going?" Q asked him.

KP stopped, looked toward a couple of guys that were looking in their direction and told him, "I was about to walk to the store right quick, give you time it make it back to the house."

"Why you park way up here instead of at the house?"

"Um, I think the motherfucker ran out of gas, 'cause it just cut off on me right when I was about to turn on the street." KP wasn't good at improvising and he knew it and therefore, switched positions with the Q&A. "Where you coming from anyway?"

"Somolia's house."

"Oh yeah?"

"You know that bitch ain't going anywhere. Get in, nigga."

KP knew there was no way he'd be able to carry out his plan now, 'cause not only did several people see him get in the car with Q, they were about to go to the nearest gas station and there were sure to be cameras there. "Take me to get some gas."

"Reach back there and get you a beer, nigga. Let me tell you what that fat bitch did when I went over there."

KP pushed the revolver deeper where he'd hid it, to smiled, laughed and acted as if nothing ever happened between them. For now he was going to do exactly what his wife made him promise and what Chris threatened his life about.

***

Datrina couldn't believe what she was hearing. After all the times Somolia talked about making men pay and what she'd do if certain things happened to her, she was now wanting sympathy for not being able to decide her own matters. Somolia had told them about Q's showing up at her house drunk and how he begged her to take him back and forgive him. She told them everything but the whole story.

"Are you serious, Somolia? Your fat ass always talking about how you going to punish a nigga and the power of the pussy, and here you are talking you still got feelings for Q. That nigga smashed your shit, took your money, and only wants to be seen with you when it's only the two of you around, and you say some shit like that. This new nigga you're with went and bought you a brand-new Benz, gives you shit all the time and for whatever reason, loves the shit you feed him and you're walking up in here talking about Q! You're a stupid bitch."

"See, you've got to understand, Datrina. Me and Q have history, we know each other in ways other people don't and although we're always into it, I know he still cares for me. He—"

"Fuck him, Somolia," another woman said. The woman went on, "You have a good man and you're going to fuck him off behind a bullshit-ass nigga that continually fucks over you."

"You need to be trying to look out for yourself, Somolia," said another.

Somolia closed her eyes. "Y'all don't understand. I'm not saying I still want to be with Q, I'm just saying I still care for him and I can't deny that, I want to be with Buddy and—"

"Buddy?" Datrina asked, stopping Somolia in the middle of her spiel. "Buddy?"

Somolia sighed. She'd slipped, but now that the cat was out of the bag, everyone took turns rubbing it.

"I hope you're not talking about Boss Lady's Buddy," said one of the women that frequented the shop and knew of him.

"That giant-ass man?"

"Yes, yes and yes," Somolia walked from her station and sat in the swivel chair next to Datrina's.

"This fat motherfucker lying, y'all," Datrina told them. "That nigga too damn big for her."

"That's what I thought until he got to stretching my shit just the way I liked it." Somolia smiled at the lot of them.

"You fucked him, Somolia?"

"He is my man. It ain't like I'm just walking, pointing niggas out and fucking them," she said, defending her actions.

"You fucked that big-ass man?" another beautician asked, still not believing what she was hearing.

"More than once and if it's any consolation to y'all, things are getting serious between us," Somolia told them.

"But, you can't decide what you should be doing? Bitch, please." Datrina went back to doing what she was doing. There was nothing to discuss, now that she knew Somolia had been keeping things from her.

"Just be real with him, Somolia. Don't fuck off a good thing because you feel as if you can't trust him to understand your situation," said one of the beauticians.

Datrina rolled her eyes at her friend and asked, "What the hell you over there looking at me for? It's evident you didn't want me knowing your business, so let's keep it that way."

"You're tripping like that, Datrina?" Somolia gave her a questioning look.

"There's nothing to trip on, Somolia."

"Oh, this bitch mad because I wanted to make sure I had something real before I brought it to the family. I wanted to make sure I wasn't just setting myself up, Datrina."

"Shut your fat ass up, Somolia. You meet a nigga at the gas station, suck his dick and run up in here talking about getting married and shit, and now you twisting your lips to say some shit like that. Fuck you."

Somolia walked over and hugged Datrina from the back. "I'm sorry, babe."

"Get your shit off of me, Somolia, it feels like you humping a bitch."

"If I was humping you, your ass wouldn't be going home to Chris every night. Your black ass wouldn't even own any clothes." Somolia ground her stomach into Datrina's ass, making her and the rest of the women laugh. Temporarily, Somolia forgot her own troubles.

***

By the time King knocked on her door, Nava pretty much knew what she was going to do and say. She greeted him with a warm smile, and even warmer hugs.

"Glad you finally showed," she told him before allowing him inside.

"Well, I did say I would stop by for a minute or two."

Nava walked him into her living room and pushed him down on the recliner that sat directly in front of the sofa. "You've had me waiting all this time, just so I can get myself off." She stood in front of him, pulled her t-shirt over her head and threw it on the sofa besides him.

"You're the one who insisted I come here to watch. You could have done this without me knowing," he told her.

She placed one foot on the sofa beside him, scooped the remote from the table and once the sounds of Prince's song "Do Me Baby" surrounded them, she threw the remote down and slowly began gyrating her hips. "You remember when I used to do this for you, King?"

"Yes, Nava," he told her without enthusiasm.

"You don't miss it?" Nava spun, put her back to him and bent at the waist. She watched him from between her legs while slowly slipping her fingers in her pussy, over her lips and down each thigh. She needed for him to see how wet she was.

"Is this what you wanted me here for, Nava?"

"This and more," she told him, before facing him and climbing onto his lap.

Where this at one time roused the hell out of King, he now simply watched her. Her once short and thick frame had been reduced to a bony structure of the woman she once was. He could actually see her ribs while her back was to him. He could see her clavicles protrude and her once firm and tight ass cheeks now sagged slightly. She might have even excited some guys while doing her dance, but his mere remembrance of how she used to be made it hard for him to find her act attractive. "Nava, will you hurry up!"

"I want you to watch me come, babe."

"Hurry up, then."

She paused, lay on the floor and spread both her legs so that her left was on the floor and her right was being held up with her hand, then she inched toward him. "Pussy still pretty, ain't it?'

"You're all right."

Nava smiled, seeing him swallow. He couldn't take his eyes off of her. "Remember this, King?" She began spanking her clit with three fingers, rubbing her pussy lips with wet hands and moaning her pleasure. She watched him adjust himself. "You like that?"

"Will you hurry up!"

Nava squeezed her clit between her fingers, spanked it repeatedly and when she felt her orgasm coming, she told him, "Get the towel, get the towel."

"Don't shoot that shit on me, Nava."

Nava fell onto her back, placed one of her nipples in her mouth and massaged her clit harder, faster. "Ummm, aghhh. Shit!" she exclaimed just before a stream of come shot from between her legs. She massaged the nut between her thighs, pussy and ass before placing fingers in her mouth. "Ummm, King, tastes like candy, babe."

King watched her come. He watched her legs shake, all the while thinking about Diamond and the morning they shared. Diamond was far from a stripper, but she'd done some things he couldn't help but remember. He was watching Nava, but thinking about Diamond. "Turn over, turn over right quick," he told her, remembering what Diamond had done. "Open your legs, put your feet together and look back at me. Fuck yourself like that."

Nava did exactly as he instructed. She was liking the way he was getting involved.

"Do it faster. Play with the clit, squeeze them thighs, pop that pussy." King had been wanting to replay the scenes from this morning all day and couldn't wait to get back with Diamond. He told her, "Act like you riding a nigga. Look back at me, twerk it real slow."

"Give me some of that dick, nigga. Fuck all this posing and shit." Nava stood and grabbed King's hand. She wanted to feel something inside of her. "Come on."

"I thought you just wanted me to watch, Nava? That's all I came to do."

"I want you to fuck me like you used to, King."

King stood, grabbed her t-shirt and handed it to her. He checked the time on his watch. "I have to go, Nava."

"You what?"

"I have something to do tonight."

She snatched the shirt from him and threw in on the sofa. "You're probably trying to go be with that bitch."

"Thanks for the show though."

Nava had a moment to seize and she went for it. "Break bread then, nigga. Pussy ain't free. Besides, I need some money anyway."

"I just gave you some money after we went grocery shopping, Nava. What happened to that?" King reached for his pocket.

"Clothes, nigga. I'm not some cheap bitch, King. You keep that bitch looking good and I want to look good too."

Telling Nava that Diamond had her own money was something he didn't do because it would only begin an argument and he wasn't there for that. "Here." He handed her fifteen hundred-dollar-bills.

Nava frowned. "What am I supposed to do with this, King?"

"Nava, that's—" he stopped himself and handed her one thousand dollars extra. "I forgot about the dance and the show you gave me." King smiled and made his way for the door. "I'll get at you later, Nava. Be careful."

"Fuck you, King. And, fuck that bougie bitch you running to too."

As soon as King left, Nava went to check the recording she had. She watched it from the beginning. She smiled, this would definitely be used. "Let's see how that Diamond bitch like seeing her mind do a little tricking," she told herself, before slipping into the t-shirt he handed her and making her way to the kitchen. To her saucer full of cocaine.

***

Chris had been talking non-stop ever since they left the McClendon Estate. He admonished her for lying to Dell about her brother wanting to move his money, because there was no way he'd be able to explain that he had nothing to do with it. Diamond was making a call he was sure had repercussions but as always, he was going to ride with her. "I'm serious, Diamond, you should have talked to your brother about it first."

"I'll tell him this weekend when me and Camille go visit him."

"Camille? King's girl?" Chris shook his head. "Hell naw, that nigga gonna be tripping on me for real then."

"He's already met her, Chris. He's actually looking forward to seeing her again."

"Really, Diamond?"

Diamond looked over at him and smiled. "Really."

Chris was just about to go off on her, but was stopped short when pulling up to the property he and Diamond came to buy. Two guys stood by a maroon Escalade—apparently awaiting their arrival.

"Punk-ass nigga still ain't here," she told Chris as he parked. Diamond climbed out of the Bentley, wearing a wide-legged pant-suit. The black-laced strapless bra complimented her breasts from under the plunging neckline of the suit. Her hair was pulled back into a single braid that hung to the middle of her back. The three-inch Dior heels she wore boosted her five foot ten frame to towering heights. Chris laughed when seeing the realtors frown at her.

"He'll be here. The way you tied him up in game, I'm surprised the nigga ain't in the trunk."

Diamond allowed Chris a formal introduction. She walked slowly towards the group.

"How's it going, fellas?" Chris shook their hands before turning and introducing Diamond. "This is Ms. McClendon."

Diamond nodded.

"Nice to meet you, Ms. McClendon." Both men nodded also. "Um," one guy began, "this is one of our most requested properties." The guy led them to the house by way of a winding sidewalk, parting a neatly manicured lawn that continued to climb.

Diamond watched the guy as he typed in the security code of the house. She knew that would be the first thing they'd change.

"This is a Victorian-styled mini-mansion. It's—"

Diamond cut him off and asked, "What makes it a mini-mansion?"

"Um, that's just a term we use when the property isn't as large as the others we sell. This particular house is seven thousand, six hundred and fifty square feet. It has four bedrooms, a guest suite, game room, indoor pool and Jacuzzi, a four-car garage, surveillance system, and that's just to name some of the perks."

"Am I late?" Dell asked from behind the group.

They all turned to face him.

"Not at all. Want to view the house also?" The realtor looked from Dell to Chris as if he was about to start a bid.

"Um no," Dell nodded towards Chris. "I'm here on their behalf."

Diamond stayed behind the men as they toured the house. She'd already decided they'd be leaving with the keys and moving Datrina and Chris the following weekend. She even had a couple of ideas when it came to the décor of certain rooms within the house. This one fit Datrina just right.

"And, the asking price is?" Dell asked, knowing they were out of their range.

"We're asking one point four million dollars. This property is highly sought out and I'm more than sure it will be bought before the week is out."

Dell stammered. There had to be a way for them to rub each other's back. "H-how many owners has it had?"

"One previous owner. This house was built four years ago."

Diamond had heard enough. She looked over at Chris, who had ventured off into the living area and stood before the wall to ceiling glass windows. "I'll tell you guys what." She snapped her fingers, getting Chris's attention. She nodded towards the entrance of the house. "I have one million dollars cash on hand and know this house was a foreclosure. The previous owners only owed six hundred thousand dollars, but due to unfortunate circumstances, they didn't pay. The way I see it, you guys will be able to pay that and some and still walk away with lined pockets. You'll easily make over a hundred thousand dollars apiece and that's more than either of you have made since you've been working for that company." Diamond smiled.

Chris walked in and dropped two duffels filled with money at their feet and unzipped each. He knew by the way they eyed the money that it was the most either of them had seen at one time and knowing how Diamond worked. He stepped back, put his hands in his pockets and looked on.

"Um," one of the guys laughed, unable to contain his surprise, "you've done your homework, huh?"

"When spending these kind of numbers, you would also." She held out her hand.

"Oh yeah—looks as if you guys are the proud owners of a mini-mansion," he told them, before placing a set of keys and a piece of paper in her hand.

"Nice doing business with you guys," Dell told them reaching for the papers he brought.

Chris followed Diamond outside, leaving Dell to do paperwork. He told her, "Ou, bitch. You lie your ass off, Diamond."

"Fuck them hoes, Chris. They lucky we got shit to do."

"Thanks, sis."

"I ain't did shit for you, nigga. That was for my girl."

"Yeah, right."

Chris walked around to the driver's side of the car and told her, "I'm going to put a home treat in this bitch."

"The hell you are. You ain't finna have this motherfucker smelling like guest and ass." Diamond pointed at him and laughed. "Or, should I say sweat?"

"Fuck you, trick."

***

Inside the National Bank was where both Dell and Raymond had most of their business meetings and therefore, he was no stranger to the employees that worked there. He had no problem getting access to either of their boxes, but had to question whether they were the correct ones when he finally did get to see inside of them. He'd collected three point three million dollars from Dell's house and was looking at a total of five hundred and seventeen thousand dollars. He wanted to laugh, but couldn't. Dell had been in charge of the finances ever since Antonio got knocked and where there was over seven million dollars in cash at various locations, only a fraction of it could be accounted for. His and Dell's job was to invest the money Antonio left them. Buy, flip and sell were the principles they were to go by and it was now obvious that other things were being done. He called Dell.

"Yeah."

"Motherfucker, where you at?" Raymond asked him, while walking out of the bank with the money they had there.

"I'm closing this deal for Chris. Doing paperwork now."

"There was only a combined five hundred and seventeen thousand dollars at the bank and I took three point three million from your house. Where is all the money, Dell?"

"Motherfucker, I told you I had some things in play and was waiting on a return."

"What things in play? The way you've been talking, I thought I was going to be looking at over ten million. You been fucking off this nigga's money, Dell."

"Y'all the ones that's been fucking off money. Y'all—"

Raymond laughed. "No need to explain the shit to me. Tell it to Antonio." There was no need in going back and forth with Dell over what he already knew was happening. It didn't take a rocket scientist to see where the money was going, and Raymond wanted it to be understood he had nothing to do with them misappropriating funds.

***

Diamond and Chris were halfway back to Fort Worth when Raymond's call came through. She showed Chris her phone screen before answering. "What's up, Raymond?

"I'm looking at a couple of dollars over three point eight million dollars."

"Well, then you need to keep looking, because there has to be some more somewhere." Diamond looked at Chris with raised brows.

"That's what I was thinking."

"I knew something wasn't right about the way he always wanted to keep the books out of the meetings we held."

"What about assets. What do those look like?"

"I've yet to look in that direction. All I know is that the cash ain't right."

"Well, check that out and get at me. I'm about to see what kind of money this nigga got personally," she told him, before ending the call.

"Where you want me to take this money?"

"You hold onto it until I decide otherwise. I want you to flip it."

"I'll try."

Diamond shook her head. "Antonio's going to kill Dell if he's fucked his money off."

"Maybe he's got it tied up in a bunch of shit. You know that nigga buy damn near everything he thinks he can flip."

"Yeah, that still doesn't give him the okay to fuck off my brother's money." Diamond found Dell's contact and told Chris to be quiet.

"Who you calling now?'

"*Shh* means shut the hell up, nigga."

Dell answered. "Congratulations, Diamond."

"There's one more thing I need for you to do, Dell."

"Yeah, what's up?"

"I want Chris to have a surprise in the garage when he opens it." She looked out of her passenger's side window.

"A surprise like what?"

"A black Range Rover. Call me once it's done." She hung up and cut her phone off. With all the money missing, she was certain he'd be able to make that happen.

"Datrina's going to love that house, Diamond." Chris smiled at her.

"You think she'll let me fuck now?"

They both laughed. Diamond, because she'd finally got Chris to get her friend out of the loft she'd been living in, and Chris because he didn't know if Diamond was for real or not.

Nicole Goosby

CHAPTER TEN

"You did what?" Camille threw her shades on the kitchen counter. She couldn't believe King's actions when it came to Nava.

"That's pocket change to us and besides, she earned it." King thought she'd be more understanding when it came to his ex, but he'd forgotten he wasn't talking to Diamond.

Camille spun towards him, placed a hand on her hip and asked, "Where are these trees you're pulling money from, because every time you go around this bitch, you're giving it away. Does she ever give you any?"

King grabbed a fruit juice from the refrigerator and walked past her. "As a matter of fact, she's thinking about managing a strip club."

Camille followed him. "A strip club? Are you serious, King?"

"She wants to open up one. You know she's used to running them and she wants to open one here." King sat, threw an arm over the back of the couch and looked at Buddy, who'd been texting for the past five minutes.

"And, I take it you're supposed to know of the perfect spot for her?'

"She wants me to front her the money to open it," he told her before turning up the bottle he was nursing.

Camille walked to where she was directly in front of him. She pointed. "Nigga, you need to be investing in something that's investing in you—not a bitch that's cashing the investment in. You've given this drug addict over four thousand dollars in a matter of days, and over forty thousand dollars since she's been back. When does the shit stop, King?"

King wanted to tell her about the little show she put on for him but that thought flew out the window minutes ago. From now on he'd just keep his interactions with Nava to himself. Him and Diamond.

"That bitch is as transparent as a marbled dildo, King." She walked away from him, thinking of the words she'd just said and stopped. Camille frowned. "Is she fucking you, King?"

King sighed, "I am not fucking her, and you know that."

"I asked, is she fucking her, and you know that."

King turned his lips at her, looked towards Buddy, who was staring at him the same way Camille was, and shook his head. There was no need in answering that question.

Camille clapped her hands three times, gaining the big guy's attention. "Can I speak to you for a second?"

***

With no place in mind, Raymond drove. For a year, he and Dell had been pretty much doing their own thing, and the need for putting up money was something they all entrusted Dell to do. Now that he needed to secure nearly four million dollars in cash, he couldn't think of a place that he felt was quite safe. He'd have to wait when it came to depositing money in a checking or savings account, because of the amount. He couldn't leave it in either of his cars, because of what happened to KP and he wasn't about to have it sitting up in his home. He could think of only one place and that was the reason he was pulling in front of Silvia's house.

"No, Raymond," she told him, hearing of his reasons for being there. KP had left not too long ago, and she really didn't know when he was coming back. Hell, she hadn't even gotten dressed yet.

"I'm out of options, Silvia. It's Antonio's money and it just might be all he has." Raymond looked down at her pleadingly.

She looked him over, noticed the duffels he was carrying and gave in. She stepped back, opened the front door wider and told him, "Close the door behind you."

"You don't realize the burden you just lifted from my shoulders, Silvia."

"And you don't seem to give a damn about the one you dropped on mine."

Raymond followed her until they were in her entertainment room. She closed her robe around her and took a seat on the sectional in the middle of the room. "No one's going to ever think you'd be sitting on millions of dollars here."

She rolled her eyes at him. "If I didn't know any better and if it wasn't for all the money in them bags, I would have sworn you came by for some of this pussy, Raymond."

He laughed, sized her up and said, "Unfortunately, that's not the case right now." He sat across from her.

"Silvia!"

She and Raymond looked towards the approaching voice. She closed her eyes.

"Silvia, I—" KP stopped at the doorway. He looked from Silvia to Raymond, then back to his wife. On top of all the things he was dealing with and had been, this was thrown on his plate also. He'd left home earlier, intent on killing a man and no sooner had he left, than another man pulled up for doing some of the same things. KP's vision turned red, all he saw was death. *He pulled the revolver from his pocket and pointed it at Raymond. "Can't leave her alone? Can't you? You just refuse to leave my wife alone." He walked towards him.*

"I love her, Kevin."

"That's my wife, nigga! That's my pussy!"

Raymond stood and told him, "I've been fucking her for years, nigga, and I'm not going to stop. I—"

Kevin fired twice, hitting Raymond in the chest and shoulder. "This is my pussy, motherfucker!"

"You're going to kill me over some pussy, nigga? When you go to prison, she's going to be fucking somebody else."

KP fired two more shots into Raymond and stood over him. His wife's voice could be heard in the background. He couldn't leave any witnesses and he knew it.

"Kevin!"

"Hunh?"KP blinked, saw the both of them staring at him as if they could see his thoughts.

"Where'd you go?"

"Um, I made a stop. I—"

"Well, we have a problem," she told him.

"What's up?" KP went to sit beside his wife. He placed his arm around her, really hoping Raymond would see they were back on good terms. KP kissed her lips. "What's up?"

"We're going to need you to purchase equipment for the new salon," said Raymond, getting to the business of things.

"Just let me know when, where and how and I'm on it," he told them with alacrity.

"It's about time and we need to get everything Somolia's going to need. Silvia already has the three hundred thousand dollars to do so, so that shouldn't be a problem."

Silvia leaned over into her husband's embrace. "We need for you to use some of your contacts to ensure we get some good equipment at fair prices."

KP nodded. He understood.

***

Dell had driven past the Land Rover dealership many times, thought better of it for wanting a certain level of luxury but as he parked, he saw a selection of fine automobiles. Automobiles he could see himself owning. He parked and climbed out of his Bentley.

"How's it going today?"

Dell faced the young salesman and nodded.

"Are you looking to own or lease?"

"That depends on how you're talking." Dell smiled before extending his hand. The salesman couldn't have been over twenty-five years old and he was pretty sure he'd be able to get the better of the deal before leaving. Without the money he normally had and used, Dell thought about the statements of his accounts. He personally had under half a million dollars and now that Diamond was insisting on a present for Chris, he was about to come out of pocket with that. The power he once had, had been taken away and the millions he once played with now gone and it was all because of Diamond. "Let's look at some of your used Range Rovers for a bit."

After being led to the front of the lot towards the pre-owned selections, Dell was hoping that with added accessories and the likes, Diamond would look past the fact that the truck wasn't new and wasn't selected from the show room floor.

**

As soon as they turned onto Silvia's street, Diamond nodded. "It looks as if she's already got company," she told Chris, seeing Raymond's Roll Royce in the driveway.

"We're right on time then."

"Knowing this bitch, she's naked right about now."

"I thought KP moved back home?" Chris said. He'd already told KP what the deal was and being that he hadn't noticed anything different concerning him, he was hoping he hadn't tripped out again.

"And, what's that supposed to mean?" Diamond looked at him prosaically and added, "That ain't never stopped her."

Diamond was surprised to see KP answer the door and before he could even greet the two of them, Diamond pushed him in search for her cousin. "Where's Silvia?"

"She's in the entertainment room," said KP, before following the two of them inside.

Silvia smiled when seeing her younger cousin and Chris. They were right on time. "You two must have been reading my mind."

Diamond looked at Raymond and told Silvia, "I doubt it."

"We just left Irving and decided to swing by here to see what you were up to," Chris added. He watched as KP snuggled up to his wife, looking as if they were the couple of the year.

"So, what's up?" Diamond fell onto the sectional next to Raymond. She eyed him.

"I brought the money here." Raymond pointed towards the duffels.

Seeing what looked like a few dollars over what she was used to spending, Diamond stood and walked over to the first duffel. "You've got to be shitting me."

"I told you over the phone what I was looking at."

"He's going to kill y'all." Diamond laughed. "Y'all some dead motherfuckers, Raymond."

Chris lowered his head, hearing Diamond's truth. There was no way around it and now that Diamond went and put their fingerprints on stolen or lost money, the same was probably true for him as well.

"Well, you already know I'm not at fault. I haven't—"

Silvia stopped him. "You're good, Raymond. I got you."

KP frowned, but remained silent. His wife was vouching for another man, when she wouldn't even pull him out of the fire. He looked towards Chris.

"She ain't going to be able to help you, nigga." Diamond pointed towards the money. "You've got to flip that shit, nigga. At least double what's there."

"I'm going to do what I can," Raymond exhaled. The weight he'd given Silvia now returned to him.

"KP's going to make sure the new salon gets the equipment it needs and whatever else that needs to be done." Silvia smiled at her husband.

"I got it. I got that end," he assured them.

"I want Somolia's grand opening to be Totally Awesome worthy. I want no expense spared when it comes to it." Silvia looked around the room at the players that surrounded her. As much as she wanted and needed to do otherwise, she knew they needed her. After looking at Diamond and hearing and seeing the power she now had, she smiled. "From now on, Diamond will be taking my place. So—"

"Bitch, I'm taking *my* place," Diamond shot back.

"Anyway, Diamond is taking my place, because I can't keep going through this shit. After Somolia's grand opening, Kevin and I are taking a much-needed vacation." Silvia smiled at her husband.

"You've been saying that shit for the longest." Diamond tsked, snatched the remote from the end table beside her and turned on the 115-inch wall unit.

"Where y'all going?" Raymond asked her, while looking at KP.

"Wherever she wants," KP added, liking the fact that his wife was including him in any event.

"The question is, who's funding this vacation?" Diamond asked KP.

"Diamond!" Chris admonished his friend.

"Diamond, what? That nigga ain't got no money."

"I got money," Silvia cut in, defending her man.

"I've got money too and when you guys get things straightened, I'm going to throw in a little something to go with it." Raymond smiled knowingly. He knew any contribution would be repaid.

"Well, whatever. Chris and Datrina will be moving in their new home this weekend and I want it to be special for my girl."

"You know we've got her, Diamond. Doing things for either Datrina or Somolia is a non-issue," Raymond assured her.

Silvia looked over at her husband. "Humph."

"What?" KP knew what she was insinuating. "What?"

Diamond wasn't about to let the chance pass her. "You know what, nigga. Keep your dick out of Somolia's mouth."

"Diamond!" Chris stood. It was time for them to go.

"She ain't said nothing wrong, Chris. Her bitch ass finally said something I agree with." Silvia laughed.

***

The inside of the Gentlemen's Club was dark and reeked of some kind of marijuana. The steady bass-line vibrated the tables and booths around them and Nava bobbed her hand and sang along with the tunes of Jeezy's "Ballin" song. She yelled from the corner booth they sat. She and a couple of her friends had been there for a couple of hours and now that they'd snorted several lines, drank a whole bottle of Ace of Spades and slapped a few asses, she was feeling herself in the worst way. They all were. "Show a bitch that pussy," she told the youngster she'd called over for a lap dance.

"We turned up in this bitch, Nava!" one of her friends yelled over the deep bass. He snorted a line and handed the bill to Nava.

"This is how a bitch supposed to work," she told him while sticking the bill up the youngster's pussy. Nava took a swig from the bottle and stood. "Let me show these hoes how to get some paper." Nava made her way to the center stage. She'd generously tipped the bouncers and knowing she had to make that money back, she walked onto the stage. With this being her old stomping ground, the DJ put on her song and when the sounds of Rihanna's "Wild Thoughts" blasted through the speakers, both guys and women rushed the stage to see the veteran perform.

***

As soon as the last of the beauticians left and Somolia and Datrina were alone, Somolia looked up at the clock. She'd texted Buddy twice within the hour to see what he had planned for the night, because of what she was going through with Q. She wanted him to know that he stopped by her house and forced his way inside. She wanted to be truthful with him and wanted him to understand the position she was in.

"That clock is going to continue to do what it does, Somolia. You need to be doing the same."

Somlia exhaled. "I texted him twice already. He hasn't returned my last."

"Where is he?"

"He said he was working."

"Call him. Just let him know you need to talk."

"I should just wait until he comes over."

"And, what if word gets to him about you and Q before you do? Then what?"

"I—" Somolia began.

"I my ass, Somolia. Call him."

Somolia grabbed Datrina's phone. She didn't want Buddy to see her number and avoid her for whatever reason.

"Put it on speaker with your fat ass. I want to hear what he says."

Somolia dialed his number. "Nosey ass."

***

Buddy had been following the black Town Car from Oak Cliff, all the way to the north side. He waited until Nava and company walked into the Gentlemen's Club before going in himself. Having found a nice cozy spot by the bar, Buddy ordered a Sprite and water and watched. He'd texted Somolia and Camille to let them know he was working and with Nava having so much fun, Buddy made sure he got recorded footage of just that. He'd walked up to the stage and threw a couple of bills, just to get a better view of all the excitement.

Still seated at the bar, his phone chimed and not being able to recognize the caller, he answered, "Yeah?"

"Hey, babe, you still working or what?"

"For right now. What's up?" Buddy signaled for the barkeep to bring him another water and Sprite.

"I need to talk to you about something important."

"Whose phone are you on?"

"My co-worker's. My battery went dead and I had to use hers."

"Can it wait until I get to you?"

"So, you're coming home tonight?"

Buddy laughed. "Why not?"

"Well, I'll see you at home."

"Give me about an hour or so." Buddy hung up and went back to recording the stripper they called "Lava Nava."

Somolia ended the call and looked at Datrina with wide eyes. "Yeah, bitch, that was a club he's at."

"It sure sound like it."

"You think he's with another woman or something?"

Somolia thought better of it. "Naw, he might be bouncing, though."

"Bouncing?"

"Yeah, bitch. Bouncing."Somolia walked back over to her station.

"That nigga done spent over one hundred thousand dollars on your fat ass and you talking about he bouncing. The big-ass nigga might be stripping."

"Shut up, Datrina. If anything, he owns the motherfucker."

"Well, you just make sure you tell him the truth when he does show up." Datrina went to make sure all the power was off before they left.

Somolia smiled to herself. She'd definitely talk to Buddy tonight, because there was no way she was going to lose him. "What the hell is he doing at a club?" she asked herself, knowing he wasn't that type.

CHAPTER ELEVEN

Camille watched the exchange between brother and sister. She might not have known things in detail, but by the way Antonio was staring at Diamond, it was obvious that something was done without his consent and knowledge. She fingered the drink before her before asking, "Does anyone want anything from the vending area?"

"Thanks, Camille, but I'm good," Antonio told her, still not taking his eyes off his sister.

"I'm straight too," said Diamond.

Camille regarded Antonio with a sympathetic expression while standing. She was really hoping he didn't go off on her because of her actions or the things he was hearing. Either way, this part of the visit was none of her business.

"What?" Diamond asked, breaking the silence between them.

"Four million dollars, Diamond?"

"Yeah."

"And, you're serious right now?"

"I told Raymond you were going to kill them. I—"

"I left them niggas over seven million in cash and all they've done is spend my shit?"

Diamond glanced around to see who might be looking. She told him. "Nigga, why you raising your voice at me? You know I didn't have shit to do with it."

"I find that hard to believe, Diamond. There's no way they'll—"

Diamond cut him off. "Motherfucker, I'm scoring my own shit with my own money and taking the losses that come with it. I'm flipping money, bro, and spending only when I see the win."

"But, you feel free to spend my money, buying your friends houses and cars and shit?" Antonio leaned forward.

"I made them niggas match what Chris was spending. Hell, if it wasn't for my nigga, Chris, you wouldn't have that."

"Where is Chris anyway?"

"Getting shit ready for when Datrina gets off work. He's taking her to the house to surprise her."

"My house."

"That motherfucker nice too, bro." Diamond nodded and smiled.

Antonio gave in. He knew she was right to call that shot, because he'd have done the same things himself. He actually wanted to tell her that she'd done right in her decisions, but didn't want her to get too cocky. He knew the game and knew things happened when power was given and taken as well. One thing he was sure of was that the game had a way of repeating itself and by the looks of it, that was about to happen. "So, now Silvia has my money?"

"What's left of it."

"And, she's trusting KP after all the shit that's been going on with him?"

"The way they were hugged up the other day, it looked like it."

"Well, the last thing I need is for that nigga to start feeling himself and running off with my shit."

"You know he's known for fucking something up and off."

"He ain't worse than any of them other niggas."

Diamond acknowledged Camille's return with a smile and asked her brother, "Where you want me to put the rest of the money?"

Antonio pondered the thought, then looked over at Camille. He nodded.

"Am I missing something here?" Camille asked, seeing the both of them eye her.

"I need you to do a little babysitting for a while." Antonio smiled.

Camille looked over at Diamond and asked, "Babysit who?"

"It's a *what* and it's about four million dollars in cash."

"I'm not sure I want that responsibility."

"Diamond will even pay you."

"What?" Diamond looked askance at Antonio.

Antonio shrugged. "You calling shots on my shit so I don't see the problem in me calling shot on yours."

"Nigga, I did you a favor."

"And, I need for you to do me another one." Antonio watched her, needing for her to understand.

"I'm not going to charge you to do that, Antonio. I more than understand your situation and I'm willing to do what you need me to. Besides, you already owe me." Camille winked at him.

"Owe you for what?"

Camille and Antonio watched each other with knowing expressions. There was no need in including Diamond in what was already fixed with them.

"Oh, you motherfuckers playing me?"

They laughed.

***

Chris had been racing against time ever since dropping Datrina off at the salon. He wanted things perfect by the time she got off, because he was bringing her home. They'd all act as if nothing had changed and once she opened the door to their loft, everything would be gone and he'd act as if they had been robbed. It was a long shot, but it was something he'd been wanting to do for the longest.

Not only did he have the movers working non-stop to clean out the loft, but he also had guys picking up the things he'd ordered for the house. Diamond made sure everyone paid their dues when it came to setting her friend up. She shelled out two hundred and fifty thousand dollars. Silvia and Somolia patched up and put together a hundred thousand dollars for the cause. And, Chris was trying to spend all of it in a matter of hours.

"Are you sure she doesn't know where you are?" Silvia asked him.

"Believe me. The phone she tracks me with is in her purse and my other phone doesn't have all that bullshit on it anyway, so we good."

"You didn't tell Somolia, did you?"

Chris just looked at her. "Well, let's get this shit done. Diamond should be through here shortly. Her brother ain't going to want to look at her for too long after she tells him all that's been going on out here."

"Tell me about it." Chris nodded at a few of the movers as they passed. He told one guy, "Please don't drop the aquarium. That motherfucker cost me seven thousand dollars."

He and Silvia walked inside. They both approved of the way things were turning out. It would definitely be in order by the time Datrina called for him to come pick her up.

***

Datrina knew when Somolia was lying and this was definitely one of those times. With Somolia claiming to have told Buddy everything that was going on between her and Q, she was still uneasy about something.

"And, all he said was okay?" Datrina asked her before looking at the other women present.

"Yeah, I'm serious."

"I'll bet you anything your fat ass standing here lying, Somolia."

"What I got to lie for?" Somolia asked with a straight face.

"Because that's what you do, Somolia. The only time you tell the truth about something is on accident and by the way you over there acting all serious, it's obvious."

"Whatever, bitch. I don't have to lie to my man."

"At least you shouldn't have to," said another beautician.

Somolia was just about comment when the door opened and Q stepped inside, with a smile on his face that caused everyone to stare and Somolia to make her escape to the back.

"Where you going, bitch?" Datrina watched her friend disappear. She turned to face Q. "What's up, Q?"

"Aw nothing, Just coming to see what Somolia got up for the day."

"Oh, really?"

"You know how we do it." Q looked towards the back for Somolia.

"You know she has a boyfriend now, don't you?" Datrina saw this as her chance to yank the blanket off of Somolia's lies.

"That's what she says, but by the way she fucked me the other day, I can't tell."

"So, you and Somoliastill fucking around?"

"You know she's not going anywhere."

"Somolia!"Datrina looked towards the back hallway. "Somolia, bring your lying ass out here!"

"Why are you screaming my name like that?" Somolia walked around to her station, trying to pay Q no attention.

"Hey, babe." Q walked towards her.

Datrina stopped what she was doing and told her, "Either you tell him or I will."

Somolia looked toward her friends and lowered her head. "Listen, Q, I am with someone right now and I would like for you to respect that," she told him, hoping it would appease her friends.

"I'm not tripping on that." He tried to kiss her cheek.

Somolia stepped back, seeing the hulking figure walk into the Totally Awesome Salon.

"Oh shit," said one of the beauticians, seeing things unfold.

Buddy watched the two of them. After being told by Somolia that Q had forced himself into her house, demanding they be together and she feared he would do something rash because of her rejecting him, he'd been following Q. Now that they were face-to-face, Buddy was about to make sure Q understood the repercussions of his actions. "Is there a problem?"

Q turned to face the deep voice, only to realize the owner of it dwarfed him. Q's mouth flew open as did his eyes. He took a step backwards also.

"Buddy, what are you doing here?"

Buddy's eyes never left Q's and his hand never left his pocket. "Making sure you're straight."

Somolia quietly walked over and grabbed Buddy's arm. She pulled him toward the back hallway. "I'm straight, babe."

Once they were out of their hearing, Datrina faced Q and told him, "You might need to be finding someone else to suck your dick now, because that nigga looked like he wanted to kill your ass, Q."

Q whispered, "That's the nigga she talking about?"

Datrina looked in the direction Somolia and Buddy went and told him, "And, I advise you to remember that. You know you don't want that woman, Q. You just be using her fat ass for the shit you want and I'm not tripping on that at all, but give her a chance to have something real. Let her go, Q."

Q looked around at the women that watched him—that at one time saw potential in him and he nodded. This had been something they all spoke on and he was more than willing to bet it. It was also something he was about to use to his advantage, because he knew Somolia and by the way she was acting, she hadn't told her new friend about what they'd done just days ago and if he was right, she wasn't about to. This would be used and this was the real reason he nodded. "Well, just tell her to get at me when she can."

Once they were away from the crowd, Somolia pulled Buddy to her. She buried her face in his chest and cried. She silently cried because of the mistakes she'd made and for the one she hoped Buddy would forgive her for. "I need to tell you something, babe," she told him between sobs.

"I'm here, Somolia. I'm not going anywhere." Buddy placed his arms around her shoulders to comfort her, to assure her.

She hit his chest with a clenched first. She hated herself for what she'd done and for what she was about to do. "The other day when I told you he forced his way in the house—" Somolia wrapped her arms around him as best she could. She never wanted to let him go.

"What, babe?" He continued to comfort her. "Did he force himself on you? Did he rape you, Somolia?"

Somolia shook her head. "He did at first, but—"

"But?" Buddy felt his phone vibrate in his back pocket. He knew who was calling.

"But I gave in. We—we had sex, babe. I didn't know what else to do."

"You gave him my pussy, Somolia?" Buddy held her at arm's length. He looked into her swollen eyes. Her usually seductive eyes were now bloodshot red. He frowned down at her.

"Please, babe," Somolia cried harder. She tried to pull him to her, but Buddy stepped back. He watched her.

"He was drunk and I just wanted him to leave, babe. I promise." She lowered her face into her hands. "I love you and I don't want to lose you. I don't."

Datrina rounded the corner, saw her friend with her back to the wall and both her hands covering her face. She saw a monster of a man standing, looking down at her with a frown that told her he wasn't approving what was being said or done. Datrina walked toward them. "What you do to her?" She eyed Buddy with question.

"We all right," he told her, never taking his eyes off Somolia.

Datrina walked up and stepped between them. She was hoping he hadn't put his hands on her friend. "You need to leave, Buddy."

"No, Datrina." Somolia reached for him, but Datrina kept her from it.

"Will you please leave?" she pleaded with Buddy while she held her friend. She pulled Somolia's sobbing frame to her and squeezed her.

Buddy checked his phone and took another step back. He watched Datrina watch him. He understood.

"And, stop all this damn crying with your fat ass." Datrina hugged her friend while watching Buddy walk away. "Fuck them niggas, Somolia."

"I love him, Datrina."

"Your fat ass love everybody, Somolia."

***

King made a few early stops, before deciding to swing by Nava's to see what she was up to. He hadn't heard from her since the day before and was hoping she was all right. Seeing her car parked under the canopy of the complex, he parked, walked to her door and knocked twice. He could hear the radio blaring from inside and instead of hoping she'd heard the knock, he walked around to her patio and jumped the wooden fence. "Why the hell does she have that radio up so loud for?" he asked, before letting himself in. King stopped, seeing a guy asleep on the couch. His shirt was off and his pants were unzipped. The end table contained both cocaine and weed and by the looks of things around the apartment, it was a party at its end. He grabbed the remote and shut off the radio. King couldn't have been anymore disgusted in his life. It only took for a cop or security to uncover the scene, and he'd be in the back of someone's police car.

He continued towards the back, not knowing what to expect and with Nava's bedroom door closed, he debated on seeing what was to be seen inside. He exhaled and turned the knob. There were two sleeping forms on the bed and one on the floor. "Nava?"

It was most likely that Nava fell onto the floor some time during the night. She wore the same t-shirt and panties as the other day. Her hair was a mess and it broke King's heart. "Nava." The two forms on the bed slowly came from under the sheets and to his surprise, one was the same gold-toothed guy Nava brought to his spot the first day she arrived, and beside him was a girl that looked as if she couldn't have been a day over sixteen years old. She and the guy were butt-naked.

"King, what are you doing here?" Nava finally asked with an attitude of her own.

"Are you serious right now? I'm surprised the cops aren't here instead." He threw the sheets on the girl and looked at the guy with hate. There was no telling what they'd done to her.

"Get out of here, King." Nava wiped sleep from her eyes and tried to stand.

"This is my apartment, Nava. I pay the bills here." King pointed towards the living area. "They need to leave, Nava. Your little party is over."

King watched as both the guys and the girl got their belongings and took their leave. His heart went out to the young girl and by the way she was dressed, she had to have been a prostitute or a stripper. King couldn't believe what he was seeing. Here he was trying his damndest to pull Nava out of that life and here she was, burying another woman under it. As soon as they were alone, King grabbed Nava's arm and pulled her. "What the fuck is wrong with you?"

"Ouch, King. You're hurting me." Nava yanked her arm from his grasp and began straightening the place.

"Here I am, trying to help you get yourself together, and you pull some shit like this. What if the police would have gotten here before I did, Nava? What if someone had called the damn cops, huh?"

"It didn't have shit to do with you, nigga, so what you tripping for?"

"Nava, I don't live like this."

"It was just a little party, King, damn. You're acting like I set the damn building on fire or something."

King took in all the bottles on the table, then the opened condom wrappers and the drugs laying in plain sight. His heart fell. "If you ever do some shit like this again, Nava—" he paused, thought about what to say and told her, "—I'm going to discontinue the lease."

"You what?"

He only looked at her.

"Nigga, you ain't here with me. You stop by when you please and you're telling me what I can and can't do. You ain't my man, King."

"Did you fuck them niggas too?"

"What if I did?" Nava faced him, looked him straight in his eyes and asked, "Did you fuck that Diamond bitch?"

Before he knew it, he'd grabbed her by the throat. He shook her. "You don't ever call her a bitch again. Bitches do shit like this," he told her while looking around the apartment. "And, this ain't some shit she does." He pushed her onto the couch and made his way to the door.

"Don't ever put your fucking hands on me, King!" Nava yelled after him. She followed him to the door. She slammed it. "Faggot-ass nigga!"

***

Diamond was feeling pretty good about the way things had turned out with her brother. She knew he wasn't about to tell her so, but what was done was done and she regretted nothing. She and Camille had been talking about the game, investments and associates when she mentioned Dell's name and even though the world was small, it had just gotten smaller.

"This can't be the same guy I know."

Diamond always knew him to be egotistical and power-stricken and said as much. "The nigga thinks because Antonio is on lock that he has the run of the mill. Hell, they acted like they didn't want me to get on at first, but then I started doing numbers that surpassed their projections."

"This has to be him though. I only know of one Dell that buys and sell properties. As a matter of fact, I did some business with him not too long ago. He sold me some product for cheap and promised to get me an opening in San Antonio."

Diamond looked over at her. "San Antonio?"

"Yep, he said he knew some people there and with the market being open, it was pretty much a win-win on both our parts."

"That nigga knows I'm pushing work in that direction."

"Sounds as if we're dealing with the same guy, Diamond."

"Snake-ass nigga."

"I stopped by his place not too long ago and he was in a heated conversation with Bell. You know anything about that?"

Diamond frowned. That name definitely rang a couple of bells. "Bell?"

"Yeah, Officer David Bell. He works for the FWPS and does private security on the side."

"David Bell. I've heard that name before, but it's not coming to me right now." Diamond thought of all the events Antonio went to and the guys he employed.

"Yeah, well, years ago he caught my brother with a few pounds of weed and I had to pay him off, so those charges wouldn't see the light of day. I wasn't about to let my brother get caught up in this shit."

"I'll have to look into him later." Diamond reached for her vibrating phone, saw the unidentified caller and pressed send. She'd been waiting to hear from Chris and knowing he wasn't on his usual phone she wasn't about to ignore the call. Diamond turned the phone sideways to enlarge the screen. It was King, sitting on a small couch, with a woman on the floor between his legs. Diamond took the exit ramp and after stopping at the red light, she continued watching the video someone sent her. "Ain't this a bitch." She held the phone to where Camille could see her best friend and the naked woman masturbating in front of him.

Camille knew exactly who the woman was. She told her, "This bitch has got to go. She's always trying to—"

Diamond laughed, cutting Camille's explanation off. "Look at this bitch's knees. She could have at least put some lotion on."

Camille watched Diamond in confusion.

"He got this bitch doing everything I did. He might be with her, but it's obvious he's thinking about the shit I did to him." Diamond laughed, handed Camille her phone and headed to Irving. They had a surprise for her girl and she wasn't going to miss that. "That bitch ain't original at all," she told Camille, thinking of Nava's performance.

"So, you ain't tripping?" Camille was devastated and there was no reason why Diamond shouldn't have been.

"That nigga fully dressed, Camille. If I was her, I'd be doing the same shit too." Diamond took another look at the video, turned her head sideways and told her, "She does have a pretty pussy though."

Camille laughed, paused the video to get a better look at it and nodded. She agreed.

CHAPTER TWELVE

Datrina had been thinking about Somolia and the things she'd gotten herself into, until Chris passed their usual exit. "You missed the exit, Chris."

"Yeah, I have to make a stop right quick and since we're out, I may as well handle it."

"Nigga, you could have done all this shit. I'm tired, my feet are killing me and I need to rest my brain." Datrina sighed, held her head back and closed her eyes.

"Take your shoes off and relax. It'll only take me a minute. By the time you take a little nap, we'll be at the house."

She faced him. "I don't want to take no damn nap, Chris. I want to sit my black ass in my tub and take my ass to bed. That's what I want to do."

Chris smiled. "So, what happened to us spending a little time together?"

"Ha, considering the way I'm feeling right now, dick is the last thing on my mind."

"What happened today?" Chris saw his chance to open conversation and needed to take her mind off the fact that they were about to drive thirty minutes before they reached their destination.

"Everything. Some bitches got into it behind some shit that happened three weeks ago at Walmart."

"What happened?"

"Something about this bitch fucking with some other bitch's son and she was old enough to be his momma or something like that. I was coming from the back and they were all up in each other's faces."

"Where was Silvia and Somolia?" he asked, knowing full well where Silvia had been.

"Silvia didn't come in today, she said something about taking care of business—and Somolia's fat ass was the one brought the shit up. How she knew anything about it, don't ask me."

"That woman's always in the middle of something, ain't she?" Chris laughed. He saw she'd finally taken her shoes off and reclined her seat a bit.

Datrina turned on her side to face him. "Oh, let me tell you what she had going on today."

"I should have known."

"The bitch is a mess. Both of her boyfriends showed up and she didn't know what to do. Her fat ass is always talking about how she got niggas trained and shit and as soon as they find out about the other guy and confront her about it, she wants to run off crying like she's on TV or something." Datrina rolled her eyes and continued, "You should have seen her, Chris, she didn't know what to say."

"Who were the guys?"

"Q and Buddy's big ass."

"Buddy?"

"Yeah, Buddy. He's the one who bought her that new Mercedes after Q beat up her other one."

"She's still fucking with Q?"

"Yep. Come to find out—she's still fucking him too."

Chris took the Irving exit. "She's fucking him and Buddy?"

"That's what I just said, Chris. I had to run to the back to make sure Buddy didn't kill her fat ass."

"I know he was mad as hell. He'd just bought her a new car and come to find out she's still fucking the nigga that trashed her other one. That's some fucked-up shit for real."

"Anyway, I told her she didn't need any one of them."

Chris turned onto their street, pulled in front of the house and parked, causing Datrina to notice the million-dollar house.

"I know you didn't just bring me to one of your drug deals, Chris."

"Naw, we're just stopping by for a minute."

"We?"

Chris smiled, unable to contain it. "Yeah, come on."

"Motherfucker, I told you I was tired." Datrina saw the winding stairs and sighed. "Don't have me up in here nolong-ass time, nigga. I'm going to embarrass your ass."

"Please don't start that shit, babe. We'll only be a minute." Chris remembered the last time she called herself embarrassing him in front of company. He laughed.

"I'm serious, Chris. I'm going to shit all over myself."

***

Camille only sat and watched as Diamond and the rest of her people got things together in surprise for her friend. She liked seeing the love among them and the fact that Diamond was the reason her friend was coming home to a million-dollar house, made her think of what she wanted for herself. This was definitely love.

"Here they've come, y'all." Diamond silenced everyone and made her way to the door. She opened it just as Chris rang the doorbell.

"Diamond, what the hell you doing here?"

She and Chris led Datrina through the foyer, around the four-hundred-and-fifty-gallon aquarium and into a huge dining room.

"Welcome home, babe." Chris wrapped his arms around his girl.

"Surprise!" they yelled in unison.

Datrina looked at them in confusion. "Don't play with me, y'all. Do not play with me right now." She looked in Diamond's direction for confirmation.

"This is all yours, Datrina. This is your shit, bitch." Diamond hugged her and kissed her cheek. "Wait until you see the rest of this motherfucker."

"I hope you like it, babe."

Datrina finally laughed. "I'm telling y'all right now, if this is some joke, I'm killing all y'all asses." She looked at Camille. "Nothing personal, Boss Lady."

Diamond pulled Datrina through high arched hallways with black marble flooring, into a kitchen with twelve-foot ceilings and into her very own theatre room.

Everyone followed.

"You like?

"We're still outfitting it, but for the most part everything is on its way and should be here tomorrow," KP proudly announced.

Diamond looked back at Chris and told him, "I might be able to get some pussy now."

"Diamond!" Silvia frowned, knowing her cousin probably forgot they had company.

"Oh, I got something for Chris too." She then led them to the rear of the house and into their four-car garage.

Silvia hit the lights.

"If you don't like it, let me know. I'll have Dell take it back and get you something new."

Chris walked around the Range Rover and nodded. He knew this was all Diamond. "Thanks, sis. I owe you one."

Diamond nodded towards Datrina and winked. "Let me fuck your girl and we're even."

***

It had been two days since she'd last heard from Buddy and she'd begun thinking the worst. She called, texted and even had Datrina try and contact him. To everyone's surprise, she was even willing to give the Mercedes back in her attempt to show him that it wasn't a game between them. All Somolia wanted was her man back.

"Just leave it alone, Somolia. He'll come around when the time is right for him," said one of the women there.

"You need to be thinking about business, instead of some nigga." Datrina walked around to where her friend was sitting and told her. "You're about to have a grand opening for your salon and that outweighs all that other bullshit."

Somolia looked over the manicure she was just given. They been giving her a queenly treatment all day, hoping it would get her mind off of the things she couldn't change. "I guess y'all are right. I'm about to make the money move and I'm tripping on a nigga, huh?"

"Yeah, bitch. Power of the pussy."

"Power of the pussy," they chanted in unison.

Datrina only looked at them with her lips twisted. "Really, Somolia?"

"You didn't know?" Somolia stood, fanned her nails and told her, "I'm not even tripping."

Somolia's phone rang and she nearly knocked over a bottle of polish remover to get it.

They all laughed.

"Hello?"

"Hey, bitch. You all right?"

"Diamond?"

"Somolia?"

"Girl, what the hell you want?" Somolia looked at the women that were looking at her. She was hoping it was Buddy and they knew it also.

"Damn. I just called to see how your no-good ass was doing. Where's Datrina?"

"She's right here, looking in my mouth like she's a damn dentist or something." Somolia turned.

"No you didn't just—" Datrina went off, making everyone laugh.

"I've got good news and I've got bad news. Which first?"

"Diamond, what is it?"

"Which do you—"

Somolia stopped her. "Good, good, good news first."

"Buddy's been asking about you."

"Why hasn't he returned any of my text or calls then?"

"Because he's away on business and he doesn't have time to be fucking with you."

"And, how would you know all this, Diamond?"

"Because King's is standing right here and he told me."

"Put him on the phone then—with your lying ass."

"Hey, Somolia."

"King?"

"Umm-hmm."

Somolia knew everyone was watching her and instead of dealing with them at the moment, she walked to where she could conduct her call in private. She had to see if Buddy really inquired about her and if he was still her man.

Diamond and King had been together most of the day and she still hadn't told him about the video Nava sent her. She knew Camille had enough to say and being that she didn't see anything wrong with that, she saw there was really no need in making something out of it.

She needed to ease Somolia's weary mind and that was the reason for the call.

"You should have lied and told her ass that Buddy didn't want shit to do with her anymore. That's what you should have said."

King handed her the phone and shook his head. "Then, I would be lying to her, Diamond. Buddy's really feeling your friend and I let her know as much."

"Now you're going to have her ass acting like her pussy is platinum."

King laughed, grabbed the Bloomingdale's bag from her and grabbed her hand.

She watched him. He'd spent damn near eight thousand dollars on her so far and she knew it as from guilt—a guilt she was going to let him deal with.

"So, what's Nava been up to lately?"

King shrugged. He hadn't been to her apartment since and hadn't taken any of her calls. For now, he'd sit back and see if she really wanted to do something with herself. "The hell if I know. I'm not even wasting my time with her right now."

Diamond leaned into him as they walked. She smiled. "Maybe you should bring her to Somolia's grand opening. Let her see the moves people are making around her."

"Hell naw, something like that will definitely go over her head."

"How in the world you get involved with her in the first place, King? I mean, how are you even attracted to her?'

"Was—was attracted to her. I'm only seeing you now." He kissed her forehead.

"Is Camille still giving you a hard time about her?"

"Like you wouldn't know. But, she's not like you, Diamond. You understand shit differently. Despite the things Nava's done and continue to do, you still want the best for her, whereas Camille would rather she died or something."

Diamond wanted to laugh, but now wasn't the time. "If you need for me to do anything for her, just let me know. Maybe I should hang out with her sometime."

"No, that's not going to happen. I don't want you anywhere near her, Diamond. Not until she gets herself together." He saw the pizzeria and pulled her in that direction.

"You're feeling like a slice?"

"A slice? I want my own pizza."

***

KP was once again in his element among the workers he'd hired. They'd gutted out the building for Somolia's salon and refurbished it in a day's time. The once Office Max had been turned into a state-of-the-art salon and he was proud of the work they'd done. Ten full stations aligned the mirrored walls of the building. Somolia's office sat in the rear, facing the street and the other two offices would be used to store files and to hold photo shoots. Two seventy-five-inch flat screens sat on both sides of the main floor and ten swivel chairs were placed at each station. With everything being new, plastic and bubble wrap lay over the chairs and glass. Somolia specifically wanted the Totally Awesome logos stitched into each chair, bigger than any of the other signs in the area.

After looking over everything and making sure nothing was forgotten, KP locked up the would-be salon and left. This was the first job he'd been assigned to and was hoping it would get him more work in the near future.

CHAPTER THIRTEEN

Nava paced her apartment in thought. She'd gotten careless, reacted rashly and now needed to regain her advantage. She called King repeatedly and with him not answering her calls or even stopping by, she had to do something. The video she sent to Diamond stayed at the top of her thoughts because of it. There was something she could do to repair the damage she'd done. She'd come too far to allow things to crumble now.

"You want to hit this shit or what?"

Nava looked over at the saucer. She nodded at her gold-toothed friend. "Just make sure y'all don't fuck all my shit."

"You're over there tripping and shit. You know that nigga ain't going anywhere until we send him."

She watched them snort line after line. Maybe that's what she needed to sort out the thoughts she was having. "Give me that shit," she said while snatching up the rolled bill. Nava did two lines, held her head back when she felt the drain, and swallowed. She smiled, nodded and did another. "I might have to get closer to that bitch first. I'm thinking about working her ass."

"Hell yeah, lace some shit on that bitch and let me put this dick on her. When he gets a look at her giving that pussy up, he'll leave her alone. I'm trying to find out where this nigga keeps his money and shit." Nava pushed her friend's head. "Let me do the thinking, nigga. You just do what the fuck I tell you to, when I tell you to."

"Well then tell me what to do with this dick," he told her before pulling it out."

Nava laughed, rubbed a finger full of powder on her gums and tongue, and went to kneel between his legs. "I want you to come down my throat and then I want you to fuck me from the back. That's what I want you to do."

***

With enough work for a crew himself and enough money to compensate them, all he wanted Q to know was that nothing could stop him from bouncing back. KP liked the fact that despite what had happened to him, his wife and her team was still willing to support him. This was what he wanted to rub in this best friend's face.

"I got everything set up already."

"I wonder why she didn't tell me about the new salon."

KP shrugged. "Maybe she didn't want you to know. I mean, this is big for her and she probably didn't want you fucking things off."

"That's fucked up, ain't it?"

KP laughed. "They spent a pretty penny on it too. She's got everything up in that bitch and to be honest with you, Silvia's going to be jealous as hell."

"Why she way out there in Los Colinas?"

"Money, I'm guessing."

"Yeah, she needs to be making something, because I want some of my shit back."

Well, let me get back to putting this shit together, Q. I've been having motherfuckers trying to contract me ever since."

"Alright. Get at me later, nigga. Let me know when she's going to open it up."

***

Q didn't like the fact that KP was now making moves without him, but for Somolia to keep her salon's grand opening from him was something he didn't understand. The thought of her trying to get from under him wasn't sitting well and he wanted her to know it. He'd invested too much in her and she was going to continue to break bread. Either that, or she could kiss her new romance goodbye. He called her.

"What do you want, Q? Don't you think you've done enough?" Somolia walked back to where she could take the call in private.

"So, you weren't going to tell me about your little salon opening up?"

"I mean, what is there to tell, Q?"

"That's how it is between us now?"

He heard her sigh. She told him, "There is nothing between us, Q. I'm doing something else now."

"Bitch, you owe me now. I've been breaking bread with you for the longest and you think you're just going to up and cancel a nigga like this?"

"I owe you? Nigga, you ain't paid me back half the money I've spent on you, so you could come up. You haven't done shit but stretched out on a bitch's money and I'm through with that. My man—"

"Fuck that nigga, fat-ass bitch. He finds out we still fucking, he ain't going to be your man then."

"We're not fucking, Q, and we won't be fucking either."

"That's my pussy, bitch. Your fat ass belongs to me. You hear—"

"Bye, Q."

"Bitch, you . . ." He stopped, not hearing anything on the other end. "Hey, Somolia! Fat-ass bitch!" he yelled before redialing her number.

***

Dell had to make a move and he had to make one fast. He'd already received a call he wasn't trying to take and after hearing that more money was needed, he knew it was only a matter of time before they arrived and he didn't need them hovering over his spot. He was making his way downstairs when the doorbell rang. He checked his watch. "Damn." There was no need trying to exit the back of the house, because he still had to drive around to the front to leave. He opened the front door. "I don't need this right now."

"Don't kill the messenger, Dell. I'm just trying to sort things out, that's all."

"Well, you tell them motherfuckers I've paid all I'm going to pay."

"You know they're not trying to hear that shit."

Dell led Officer Bell inside, walked him to the living area, and offered him a seat.

"Like I was saying, Dell, these guys know you're sitting on dirty money and they feel as if you'd like to keep it that way."

"These motherfuckers shaking me down, that's what they're doing." Dell walked towards the red oak shelf and grabbed a couple of files. Properties he was trying to sell. He tossed them towards the officer.

"What are these?"

"Each of them properties could easily be sold for fifty thousand. Tell ya goons that's all I have."

"You know they not interested in selling properties, Dell. That's your area of expertise."

"That's all I have and that's all I can give, and it seems as if you're the only one sweating dollar amount anyway. I've paid the price I spoke of and every time you come around, it's always some more shit."

"These are resourceful guys, Dell. You've not only broke the law but you've betrayed the very ones that gave you access to such—" Officer Bell looked around the living area, before finding the words he was looking for. "—lavish living."

"Well, some people are able to live well off of their investments."

"My sentiments exactly. Dell, these guys feel as if they've invested in you and the things you got going on."

"That's really over one hundred thousand dollars in those files. I—"

"Cash, Dell. That's the way we've been doing business and that's the way we're going to continue."

Dell thought about the purchase he'd made for Diamond and the dent it put in his account. There was no way he'd give them a hundred thousand dollars and not be damn near broke. This was not the picture he wanted to paint himself in.

"I'll tell you what will make all of this go away." Officer Bell stood.

"And what would that be?"

"Give us King and the things you promised and it all goes away."

Dell shook his head. "I don't even know where the guy is. The lead I had on him came up empty. You motherfuckers are cops and I'm pretty sure you can get him yourselves."

"King wasn't even on our radar, until you brought attention to him. You're the one who promised us his money so you could continue to do what you've been doing, but then you are the one that reneged, Dell. You're the one that initiated all of this so you wouldn't have to deal with the fact that you—"

"I got you. I got you," Dell cut him off. He understood. "I'll have something as soon as I close on these smaller properties."

"Why don't you try to get a better lead on King first? Let's make this worth both of our time and end this shit."

Dell followed the officer to the door and saw him out. He went back and looked over several files. "God dammit!" If only he could have been the one that found Chris and Datrina's new home. If only Diamond hadn't gotten in his way.

***

Silvia and Datrina gave each other sideward glances when Somolia began telling her story. Not only was she suspect, but it was always that they'd find out other things once the shit did hit the fan. And now that she was about to have her own salon and a heavier load of responsibility, Silvia tried her best to get Somolia to understand that she'd have to rid herself of all the drama Q brought her.

"Stop playing with this shit, Somolia. These niggas ain't out here pushing reset every time you want them to. Motherfuckers out for the win and when you get caught slipping, that's on you because you're the one that put them in position."

"I don't understand all that game shit, Silvia. I—"

Datrina snapped her fingers at Somolia. She told her, "These games you've been playing with these niggas, Somolia. You know what the hell she talking about."

"I told him it was over and that I wanted to be with—"

"That's what you keep saying, fat-ass woman, but as soon as a nigga show you some dick, ya ass swings around and ya legs fly open."

"And her mouth," Silvia added.

Somolia held up both her hands and extended both her middle fingers. "I learned from you two bitches."

"Well then, learn to keep your shit closed now."

"I'm telling y'all, I'm not fucking with Q like that anymore. I'm into bigger and better. Literally."

Silvia was really hoping that was the case with her friend, because the last thing she was wanted was to find Somolia rolled up in some carpet. "Have you started screening employees yet or what?"

"Girl, I haven't had time to do shit. I've been so busy with all this other stuff."

"Yeah, shit that don't even matter, Somolia. It's time to get in the game, bitch. You've been screaming about this salon shit for the longest and now that it's happening, you're trying yourself up in some bullshit. But don't worry, I'm going to help you until you get up and running."

"We all are," Silvia chimed in.

"And, I thank y'all too."

"I already hired a few girls that just graduated from cosmetology school. I have to talk to a few more."

"I want some punks too."

"For what, Somolia? So you can become the queen of messy?" Silvia didn't understand her friend.

"She probably wants better tips about how to take it in her ass. Your fat freaky ass going to end up with AIDS, watch."

"I'm not going to be fucking the help, bitch. I got a man." Somolia smiled.

"You know them punks be having some big-ass dicks, right?"

"So, I heard," Somolia agreed.

"See, that's what I'm talking about right there." Silvia jumped up. "You let another motherfucker take over your shop if you want to. You see what Cotton was doing in Queen Latifah's shop."

"Bitch, please. We're Totally Awesome. Remember that," Somolia told them.

"There she goes with that shit."

Diamond had been thinking about some of the things her brother spoke on ever since the visit. He'd even told her he'd take care of things but as always, she wasn't the one to let things slide and since it was already something she'd been wanting to do, she wasn't about to let anyone or anything deter her from it. She pulled into Dell's estate, jumped out, and climbed the stairs. Chris might not have complained about the pre-owned gift, but that was unacceptable in her book. She banged on the huge oak door with her fist.

"Dell!"

She stepped back, looked up towards the second story and yelled, "Dell!"

"What's up, Diamond?"

"Nigga, you heard me out here."

"I was upstairs."

Diamond pushed past him. "We need to talk."

"Can this wait, Diamond? I'm on my way out."

"Whatever you got going on can wait, because I'm not satisfied with the way this shit is going."

"Excuse me?" Dell followed her into the house, down the marbled hallway and into the kitchen.

Diamond looked into his refrigerator, found nothing of interest and closed the door. "I spoke with Antonio and he had a million questions I couldn't answer."

"Diamond, look. I'm in the process of—"

"That shit is getting old, nigga. You should have thought about the process before you started fucking off my money."

"Your money?"

Diamond faced him, "Yeah, my money. Antonio left everything to me and I've been allowing you niggas to freestyle. Now that the music ain't playing, I need to see my shit."

"Um, Diamond, we have money tied up in a number of things and we—"

"In what? Let me see something tangible. Fuck all these words."

Dell handed her the files he had. "Here's a couple I was looking over earlier. These are being inquired about as we speak and if everything goes right, we'll be looking at something nice in a matter of days."

Diamond flipped through the first file. "A car wash?"

"Along with a washerteria."

She laughed. "What else you got?"

He led her to his downstairs study, pointed at more files and told her, "I've more than a few and—"

"Show me, nigga."

"What is your problem, Diamond? You come in my house, demanding I do shit for you. You talking about money that was entrusted to me by your brother years ago, and act as if I haven't been doing what I'm supposed to be doing. Where—"

"As far as I'm concerned, this is my house and until you start showing me where my money's been going, you might need to be thinking the same thing. And, being that you feel you can buy my nigga anything after I told you what I wanted for him, I need something in San Antonio, ASAP." Diamond turned her head to the side, regarded him with raised brows and awaited his answer.

"We don't have the funds to purchase anything in San Antonio, Diamond." Dell's tone sounded defeated.

"I thought you had contacts in San Antonio. I thought you were going to put me there through your people."

"I've been out of the loop for trying to do other things, Diamond. Give me a minute to see what's going on."

Diamond began walking towards the door. She told him, "Nothing fancy. And, it's not long-term."

***

Camille laughed, hearing Diamond tell her of the visit she had with Dell. She knew that would rattle his cage and was more than sure he'd start doing things to get Diamond out of his hair. The way Camille saw it, when you started taking out of a person's pocket, they'd do the unexpected and that was exactly what she wanted him to do. Camille had given Diamond the game from her end and liked the zeal she had when going about executing it. All she had to do now was bake a cake for Nava, and Camille was sure that once Diamond became the icing used to do so, Nava wouldn't be able to resist. "Now, we watch his next move."

"You should have seen him. The nigga even called himself going off on me, for wanting to see where my money was going."

"Technically, it isn't your money, Diamond."

"Well, it is now. As long my bro is in prison, I'm running this shit." Diamond laughed. "I see why Silvia's running from this shit. It takes a boss to make this shit happen."

"Your ability to make money doesn't make you a boss, Diamond. It's your ability to make the toughest decisions that places you above the rest. That's what determines your status in this game. The title 'Boss' isn't truly respected until the game gives it to you."

Camille remembered her promise to Antonio McClendon and the fact that she didn't think Diamond would heed to her words. He told her that Diamond looked at her in such regard. Now that Diamond was actuating the things she advised, she wasn't about to lead her astray. She was going to be there for Diamond until the end. "We've got to make motherfuckers move, Diamond. To get in a person's head is one thing, but to make them move the way you want them to, is the only thing."

Nicole Goosby

CHAPTER FOURTEEN

"Oh my God! Oh my God!" Somolia covered her mouth, seeing the firemen do their best to contain the blaze. She'd been called to the Irving Plaza right at three-forty a.m. and knowing something was terribly wrong, she grabbed her keys, jumped in her Benz and got there as fast as she could. Silvia and Datrina were already there when she did arrive, and they were the ones that kept her at bay when she tried running into the burning building. Her shop was to open in a matter of days and now this happened. She couldn't believe it.

"It's okay, Somolia. It's okay. They got here before any real damage could be done." Silvia stood and watched as the firemen walked in and out of the doors of the salon. They'd already informed her of the fact that another of the business owners had just so happened to be passing by the plaza, when they spotted the blaze coming from the would-be salon. And, being that the fire station was just two blocks away, they were able to save the building. The only damage done was to the tinted-glass front and doors and the first few feet into the salon. The ceiling had been burned, but because some of the material used had yet to dry, the fire didn't spread as fast as it would have, had it been dry. And for that, she and the other business owners were all grateful.

Datrina continued to look around them at the small crowd that had now gathered outside of their salon. She couldn't help but think that they'd wonder why anyone would do such a thing to a salon that was yet to open.

She knew they were now wondering who these women were, even wondering about the heat they'd brought into their establishment. Datrina heard one of the closest business owners complain about the fire coming so close to his diner, and how he didn't need his places closed because they couldn't handle their business by bringing their drama. She wanted to say something, but didn't. Somolia was doing enough crying as it was. "Something must have been left plugged up or some electricity sparked from somewhere," she told them loud enough to get other people talking about the possibility.

"KP swore that everything was looked over before he left," Silvia added, really wanting the fire to be anyone else's fault but her husband's.

"I can't believe this shit!" Somolia looked at the faces that stood around her. Someone had to have seen something or someone. "Whoever did this don't even know us," she said.

"Well, whoever or whatever didn't do good enough." Datrina checked her phone. After getting the call from Silvia, she'd rushed out of her home and forgot to tell Chris where she was going, and it was now she was answering his call. "They set the salon on fire, Chris."

"What? Where you at?"

"I'm at the salon. I've got to go. I'll tell you everything when I get home." She ended the call there and then.

Silvia acknowledged the policeman as he approached her. She was hoping he had some answers to the questions nagging in her mind. And, being that she was the first to arrive, she was the person spoken to before any.

"Mrs. Piersons?"

"Yes, I am." Silvia nodded again.

"Do you mind if I ask a couple of questions about the business you're opening here in the Irving Plaza?"

Silvia didn't know what the officer was driving at. The last thing she needed was for things to roll back on her. She told him, "She's the one opening this branch, as well as the owner." She pointed at a distraught Somolia.

Seeing him turn his attention towards the woman he now referred to as Ms. Rhodes, Silvia walked over to where she could see inside the shop. She frowned.

"What's up?" Datrina asked, noticing Silvia's expression.

"Probably nothing. I just thought KP said he put the chairs inside the building."

"He did, didn't he?" Datrina took a closer look inside also. "Ain't shit in there."

"Thank God for that," Silvia sighed.

"Luckily, the fire didn't get a chance to spread."

"Yeah, we good. We'll be up and running in no time." Silvia finally smiled. All hadn't been lost

"You think Q did some shit like this?" Datrina had been wanting to ask the question ever since arriving.

Silvia looked back at Somolia and the cop. "I would hate to think someone has some pussy that good."

Datrina slowly nodded and added, "And to think, some ass would be scaring the shit out of me." She then looked back to where Somolia stood, threw her arm around Silvia and told her, "That bitch can act though. Look how she over there tripping like she done lost everything she ever owned, like she's about to collapse and shit."

"I'm just hoping Kevin ain't the reason this fire started. You know how liable his ass can be at times."

After sharing a muted laugh, they made their way back to where Somolia held her audience. Whatever the case though, they'd soon find the person or persons responsible for the fire and it was then they would be dealt with.

***

KP went over his steps repeatedly. He remembered everything he'd done before leaving the salon for that day and one of the things he was sure of was that he personally saw to it all of the stations were set and the new chairs Somolia requested was at each station. He was also sure the equipment he and the rest of the guys left inside was stolen also. The one thing he could not shake was that he'd had a surprising conversation with Q that same day. And, by the way Q was talking, he couldn't believe Somolia would have such an event and not include him. In his mind, he wasn't about to put anything past his best friend. Not even this.

Shortly after receiving the call that they were cleared to return to the salon by the Irving Fire Marshall himself, KP had the guys up and running. He was insisting on having things down as best and as fast as he could. For now, he'd show Q that nothing he did could stop the drive he had within him.

***

Camille sat and listened to the account from Diamond's end. She was never the one to jump to a conclusion without having a pretty good idea of what was really taking place. She didn't know Somolia personally, but had a pretty good idea how the fire came about days ago.

"I try to look over the shit Q does when it comes to her, but at times he surprises me to no end," Diamond told her as they sat in Camille's studio.

King had gotten up three times in five minutes, making sure Diamond was both comfortable and had a full glass of fruit juice and it was starting to annoy Camille in the worst way.

"King!"

"What's up? You need anything while I'm up?"

"I need for you to stay seated. Please. She's not a wet napkin, King."

"I was just making sure."

"You should be very sure by now, King." Camille snorted.

"Jealous ass."

Instead of throwing something at him, she only closed her eyes. Camille wasn't about to let him get to her right now. "So how much did they take?"

Diamond looked at King and smiled. It would be nice of him to sit down somewhere, but she wasn't going to tell him. "They only took ten station chairs and some equipment. The fire didn't get to spread too much and being that it was set by cocktails, most of the damage was done right there in the front."

"What other businesses are in the area?" Camille looked toward Buddy. She knew he and Somolia were at odds at the moment, but she could also tell he was wanting to know how much everyone else knew as well.

"It's a plaza, so there's all kinds of business there."

"I might need to open up something myself," said King.

Camille only looked at him. His wanting and needing Diamond to know that he was there was causing her to wonder. "I'll tell you what, Diamond, I'm going to give you fifty thousand dollars to help your friend rebuild."

"Oh, no. We're straight. That loss wasn't—"

"I'll match that," King interrupted them both. "I like Somolia."

"Is that the only reason for your generosity, King?" Camille asked, knowing Diamond could now place his generosity elsewhere.

"Yeah, I mean, and she's Buddy's girl. Why wouldn't I throw in?" King shrugged his shoulder and stood.

"I'll give you a hundred thousand dollars," Buddy told them in his deep voice. He stood also. "I'll be back in ten minutes," he told them before leaving.

Camille watched the big guy leave. "Whatever happened to the forensics on the bullets used in the shooting that happened at Q's home?"

Diamond took a sip of the juice she was given. "Nothing. No prints, no partials, no witnesses."

"Could this be retaliation of some kind?"

"Possibly." Diamond leaned back, her thoughts taking her to a darker place. A place she'd been in a lot lately. "*For what* is the question I've been asking myself though." She watched King exit also and when they were finally alone, she told Camille, "This was just a message. No signature."

"Exactly."

***

King caught up with Buddy just as he was climbing into his truck. There was something he wanted to explain and the sooner the better. "Hey, Buddy."

Buddy lowered the driver's window. "What's up, King?"

"You know I didn't mean anything by that, right?"

Buddy laughed. "You're good, King. You're good."

"The way you walked out, I could tell that something was on your mind. You're all right?"

"Couldn't be better."

"You know Camille's worried about what you might do, right?'

Buddy nodded and told him, "Maybe it's time I paid this Q fellow a visit."

"Be careful, Buddy."

"Don't I always?" Buddy pulled off. He'd go get the money he promised and after that, there were a few more stops he'd make. He reached down in the compartment on the side of the console, made sure he had enough fire power and began loading the MAC-11.

King pulled his vibrating phone from his pocket and looked at the message it displayed. He hadn't returned any of Nava's calls or texts in a couple of days, and was really needing to see how his ex was doing. He called her.

***

Nava smiled to herself when seeing King's call come in. Since they'd last talked, she didn't know where he was mentally, and for him to be calling now, she hoped she'd gotten Diamond out of the picture. Time was of the essence and she was more than ready to get things over and done with. "Hey, babe," she answered on the first ring.

"What's up?"

"I just wanted apologize for what happened the other day. I know you mean well and you always have. I'm just going through some shit right now and I'm having a hard time sorting shit out."

"Are you alone?"

"Yep."

"Have you been doing anything?"

"Like what?"

"Drugs, Nava. Drugs."

"And, it's been a struggle not to, King. I'm trying, babe. I really am."

"So, what's up? What do you need?"

"I'm missing you."

"Nava, I—"

"You know I can't do this without you, King. You've become that lifeline for me."

"I'm kind of tied up right now, Nava. Diamond's friend is in a bind and I had to spit up fifty thousand dollars to help out there."

"Fifty thousand! Damn, King."

"It's nothing. She's trying to open her business and—"

"And you gave another motherfucker fifty grand? I could have used that money to open up—"

"Nava, we already talked about that and I'm still not opening up no strip club."

To hear that he wasn't upset about the video she sent, meant either his girlfriend didn't show him or hadn't seen it herself yet. She knew she had to play this card just right. "Where's your girlfriend now?"

"She's inside."

"So," Nava found her most seductive voice, "you just stepped out so you could return my call?'

"As a matter of fact, I was already outside talking to a friend."

"Yeah, whatever, King. Can you stop by?"

"Not today, Nava. I have a ton of things going on and I'll most likely be heading out of town later on today."

"Where you headed now?" she asked, knowing it would be drugs and money involved.

"Out of town, Nava. Why?"

" 'Cause I want to see you when you get back. I want you to surprise me, so I can show you that I haven't been partying or getting high. I've been sitting here by myself, trying to get my thoughts together."

"I'll tell you what, put something together and we'll talk later." Before hanging up, he told her, "And, nothing that sounds like a club, Nava."

Nava lowered her phone and smiled. She was still in it.

"What did he say?"

She looked down at her gold-tooth wearing friend and pushed his head back down between her legs. "He said you need to suck this pussy better." She arched her back and laughed.

***

Chris being accused of certain things would normally be the reason he sustained from certain actions, but today he was concerned with one thing and one thing only, and that was getting at Q. He'd called him a couple of times but knew conversations differed when they were held in person and that was why he was parked in Q's driveway now. The last time he was here, he'd made both him and KP a promise and despite it having nothing to do with the reason he was there now, it would definitely apply.

He knocked on Q's door twice and hearing the lock on the other side turn, he subtly pulled his knife from his pocket. "Have you seen KP?" he asked, knowing the question would throw the man inside.

Q opened the door with question. It had been a couple of days since he'd heard from his best friend and he was now hoping nothing had happened to him.

"He hasn't been through."

Before Q could finish, he felt the tip of the blade bite through his stomach. Before he could respond or defend himself, he was slammed into the wall behind him, and Chris's forearm was pinning him under his neck. He was lifted slightly off the ground.

"I am so sick and tired of you motherfuckers doing stupid shit," Chris began.

"Please, Chris. I was just messing with her, man."

"You think so?" Chris pushed the knife deeper, piercing Q's abdomen. He kicked the door shut before looking around. "Who's here with you?'

"No one, no one. I promise."

"Why couldn't you just leave the woman alone, Q? Why am I killing you because of the shit you allow yourself to do behind a woman?"

"Please, Chris. I'll leave her alone. I—"

"It's too late for that, nigga. You're fucking with Silvia's money now."

"Silvia's money?'

Chris pulled the knife from Q's stomach and watched him grimace in agonizing pain. "Nigga, I barely cut you and you acting like ya insides hanging out or something."

Q grabbed at the cut, saw bloodied fingers and pleaded, "Please don't kill me, Chris. I didn't know what else to do. I fucked up."

Chris stood there watching Q spill his confession. Pieces of the puzzle were definitely coming together. "Where the money at now, nigga?" He drew back with the knife.

"Jeff spent it, he spent it on the renovations crew he started," Q spoke as fast he could, never taking his eyes off the blade Chris held.

"All of it?"

"Damn near. He's got trucks, equipment, tools, a crew and everything. The way KP ran his is the same way Jeff's running his."

"So, you and Jeff split the money y'all stole from KP?"

"Jeff stole it. He just gave me a hundred grand and made me co-owner, in exchange for some heavy paying contracts."

"KP is your best friend, Q. How you do some shit like this?"

"I told you, man. I fucked up."

Chris understood exactly what KP was going through and was now standing in the exact position he warned KP not to. There had to have been a way for them to get past what was happening between them. One thing Chris did know was that Q had nothing to do with the fire. "Just leave her alone, Q."

Q bent at the waist. "I promise, Chris. I won't even look at Silvia again. I promise."

Chris walked towards him. He'd heard him right and he was sure of it and to make sure, he told him, "Somolia too."

"Both of them, I'm through fucking with both of them, man. I swear."

Chris backed away from him, slid his knife back into his pocket and told him, "You might need a couple of stitches for that cut and let this be the last time we have this talk, Q. I still can't believe you did KP like that."

"I fucked up, Chris, and the shit kills me every day, but . . ."

Chris shook his head. KP was right about it all. His best friend had betrayed him in such a way, it was only right to kill him. It was only right that he be dealt with.

CHAPTER FIFTEEN

Diamond left Camille's with two hundred thousand dollars in cash. She tried to refuse the money twice, but then Buddy and King began walking it to her Corvette and she wasn't about to fight either of them. If they wanted to do for Somolia, then she had to understand it. Since it was Buddy that insisted she take the money he'd given her, it was only right that she took it all. She'd already spoken with Chris and once he began telling her of all Q confessed to, it didn't surprise her one bit. When it came to the people that worked, walked in or walked out of the Totally Awesome Salon, there were no surprises.

"Ain't no telling how long they been fucking around." Diamond felt for KP. For the longest, she'd painted him as the screw-up in the marriage he and her cousin had, and she was now understanding his action.

"That's why KP's been tripping about all of this."

"And, this nigga Jeff's the one that got my money?"

"Most of it anyway. Can you blame him, Diamond?"

"Hell, yeah. That was my shit." Diamond pulled to the light, saw she had an incoming call and told him, "Let me get back at you later, Chris. Money on the line."

"Just chill on that end, Diamond. We'll handle that in due time."

"Oh, I'm not tripping on that shit with Jeff right now. I'm going to deal with his ass later." Diamond clicked over. "Sergio?"

"Young Diamond."

It hadn't even been a month since she'd last dealt with her supplier. For him to be calling now, she wondered what was up.

"You sound saddened. What's the matter?"

"Life has its way of making sure no smile lasts long and no hard time too overwhelming."

Diamond understood like he wouldn't imagine. Experience always came with his words. And, it was times like these where Diamond listened. "Were there any shorts on that issue?"

"Oh no, Young Diamond. That's not the nature of my call."

"So, what's up?"

"I know you are a woman of resources and I'm willing to compensate you for them."

"My resources?"

"I'll definitely make it worth your while."

Diamond drove through the light. "I'm listening."

***

Silvia, Datrina and Somolia conducted their meeting in the confines of her office. Arson had already been mentioned, but the reason was something they were still yet to figure out and with Somolia being involved, there was a bunch of figuring to do.

"If I find out that one of these bitches burned my shit, I'm going to catch a murder case, and I'm not bullshittin'."

"Girl, sit your fat ass down." Datrina pulled her arm. "I'm trying to think and you running around here talking about killing somebody."

"I'm serious. I don't play this shit."

"That's what we've been trying to get you do all along, Somolia. And, don't rule out the fact that you might be killing your ex-lover," said Silvia.

"Or any of your so-called friends that come up in here, just to see what you got going on," Datrina added.

"Now, I've got to buy all this shit again, because we had yet to put insurance on the building."

Silvia looked out of her office window. She watched as Diamond wrestled with the huge bag. "What in hell this woman got going on now?"

They all looked towards the window.

"Ain't no telling when it comes to her," Somolia concluded.

"Just be careful from now on, Somolia."

Diamond walked into her cousin's office, dropped the duffel at Somolia's feet and smiled. "I guess your pussy do got power."

"What are you talking about, Diamond?" Datrina began unzipping the bag.

"Some certain person insisted that I give this to her." Diamond walked towards Somolia. She looked down at her. "I heard your pussy got electric currents running through it."

Somolia stepped back. Diamond had begun pressing her body onto hers and that was something she hadn't done before. "Um, you all right, Diamond?"

Datrina laughed. If anyone knew Diamond, it was her and touchy-feely was definitely a way to describe Diamond at times.

"Don't run now, bitch. I'm trying to touch this pussy that's got niggas spending two hundred thousand dollars in cash on."

"Two hundred thousand dollars!" Silvia walked from around her desk to look inside the bag also. "Who the hell you get this from?"

"Somolia's boyfriend and his friend, and his best friend."

"What? Boss Lady gave you this?" Somolia's mouth flew open. She still hadn't spoken with Buddy but here he was, doing what he continually did.

"And, you running around here sweating Q's broke ass. Your fat ass got a gold mine, but you steady digging in"

"I told y'all I don't fuck with him like that no more."

"You shouldn't be fucking with him at all, Somolia," Silvia chimed in.

"Well, I'll just have to see the pussy later, Somolia, because I have to make a run to Dallas."

"And since you brought this all the way here, you just tell me when. I'm even thinking about letting you touch my pussy." Somolia held up stacks of one-hundred-dollar-bills.

"Freak ass," said Datrina.

Diamond got to the door and looked back at her. "I'm going to hold you to that, Somolia."

KP was walking in just as Diamond was exiting the salon. She stopped.

"Hey, Diamond, what's up?"

"I owe you an apology, KP."

"For what?"

Diamond smiled before laughing. "Go talk to your wife and them. They have something for you."

He watched her until she'd backed out of the parking spot and pulled out of the lot. That was a first.

***

Camille understood exactly what Diamond was about to do. In fact, she was encouraging her to do so. With both of their resources combined, it wasn't hard to narrow down the playing field and get a better look at the players. This move would be the confirmation she needed. "I would have liked to travel with you, but some things we have to do alone."

"I just want to spend some time with the bitch." Diamond laughed. "I just might get to see that pretty little pussy tonight."

"You are a trip, Diamond. Your curiosity kills."

"Hm, let me print that one." Diamond ended the call.

Camille walked over to her kitchen counter and sat on one of the stools, her memory taking her back farther than she could recall. Back to when it all began and back to the ways she thought it would all end. Now that the pieces were being moved, she realized she was also being moved, at least emotionally, and that was something she hadn't thought about. And, it was also something she understood.

***

King thought he'd be able to make the trip quicker, but traffic played a bigger role and had become the determining factor when it came to it. He'd already texted Diamond to let her know that he was still on the road as well as called Camille. He even sent Nava a text, letting her know he was held up and she was to go on about her day as if it was never discussed he'd stop by. His mind was on Diamond for most of his trip and he wanted her to know it.

Diamond picked up on the second ring.

"You're missing me already?"

"You'll never know how much."

"How about you just show me when you return?" Diamond turned into the Broad Moore apartment complex and headed for the back.

"Sounds as if you're looking forward to it."

"Can I?"

"Why not?"

"Is it going to be the same things you showed me the last time you had me expecting?" She smiled at the memory.

"Nothing like it."

"Oh, really?"

"Really. I'm going to blow your mind, Diamond."

Diamond parked, checked the parking around her and told him, "Well, let me take care of some business right quick. Make sure you get at me once you're returning home."

"Are we meeting or what?"

"I just might be there waiting," she told him seductively.

"Bye, Diamond."

Diamond checked her appearance in her visor mirror before climbing out and making her way to Nava's apartment.

"Who is it?" Nava asked from behind the closed door. King had called to tell her he had other things to do and she wasn't expecting anyone else. She wiped her nose free of any powder residue before opening the door. "Diamond?" She couldn't believe her luck. This is exactly what she wanted.

"Can I come in?"

"Yeah, yeah, come in." Nava checked outside before closing the door. There was something definitely wrong with the woman she'd just welcomed into her apartment. "Are you all right?" she asked the disheveled woman.

"I think King's cheating on me." Diamond wiped her eyes with a tissue Nava handed her.

"Um, where is he right now?"

"He's probably with another woman right now. He hasn't returned my call and he's always gone."

Nava sat beside Diamond, handed her more tissue and when she was sure Diamond wasn't paying her any attention, she rolled her eyes upward. The woman was pathetic and more than anything, she was fucking off her high. "Do you want anything to drink while I'm in the kitchen?" she asked before standing. If she was able to paint the picture correctly, King would be running back to her in no time and not Diamond. You don't need all this drama. King knows you're not built for this shit."

***

Buddy had been watching Q for most of the day. He'd followed him to a couple of spots, but it wasn't until Q was walking into the bathroom of the JPS Hospital did he notice the monster of a man walking in behind him. He didn't recognize him at first, but as the door closed and he saw that they were the only two men inside, his mind stopped and he faced the guy. "Buddy?"

"Let's go have a couple of drinks. I know the perfect place."

"Um, I, what are you doing here?" Q stammered, saying the first thing he could string together.

"I had to stop by and check on some contracts with the hospital, that's when I thought I saw you." Buddy could see the discomfort in Q and to allay his anxieties, he walked over to one of the urinals to relieve himself.

"Um, yeah, sure," Q did the same. He very seldom passed up the chance to get drunk and despite the feeling in his gut at the moment, he was hoping he would get past it. "You and Somolia still fucking around or what?"

"Fuck that bitch. I fucked one more time and walked out on her ass."

"Oh yeah?" Q hadn't heard this, but was wanting to hear much more. He smiled inward, hoping it couldn't be heard in his voice. "I wanted to warn you about her that first time I saw you."

Buddy smirked. "Yeah, you should have."

"That fat bitch used to make me take that pussy. Especially when she started tripping," Q told him as they made their way outside. Buddy nodded. That was the exact reason he was here now. Q had taken his pussy.

"She's used to shit like that though. I've been taking that pussy for years now."

They laughed, climbed into respective cars. To Buddy's surprise, Q followed him to the location he spoke of. They'd have a couple of beers, a few laughs and get some things straightened. And, Somolia Rhodes was the reason.

Nicole Goosby

CHAPTER SIXTEEN

Dell sat on the stool of his mini bar. He was nursing a drink he'd been sipping on for the past ten minutes. He'd been moving so fast, he hadn't noticed the people that were watching both him and his moves. The bind he was now in was something he hadn't put into the equations he continually summed up. The Circle he once headed had all but turned their backs on him, and he was feeling it in the worst way. He no longer had the millions of dollars he recently had and was no longer able to invest or make moves favorable to him. Without the Circle and access to the money it had, Dell was broke.

He finished the drink sitting before him and sat the glass down slowly. The first thing he had to do was better position himself with the Circle and to do that he had to get back into Chanel's good graces. He'd make the trip to San Antonio himself, get with a few realtors he'd done business with in the past, make a couple of promises and deliver Diamond the keys to her very own town home. Either way, he was about to regain his status, as well as the McClendon fortune.

With a plan to put into play, he grabbed the keys to his Bentley, placed both his phones in the inside pocket of his Italian suit jacket and headed out the door. He'd see what was up with King later.

***

The paperwork had been seen many times before, but today Raymond was able to see more than what was being shown to him. Now that Dell wasn't standing over his shoulder pointing out this and that, he was looking at properties and a list of the ones Dell saw so much promise in. He nodded at a few but for the most part, nothing totaled to the amount of money missing from the investment firm accounts. It wasn't until he was looking through a miscellaneous file did he see that the four-million-dollar mansion

Dell prided himself with was purchased with McClendon money. It was one of the properties they were to sell. He phoned his boss.

"What's up, Raymond?"

"Hey, Diamond. Hope you're not busy, because I'm going to need you to sit down for this."

"What's up?"

"That house Dell's living in belongs to Antonio, and that's where most of the missing money is. I was able to go into other files and found some more properties, but that's something that stood out to me more than any."

"Tell me something I don't know."

Raymond chuckled, "So, you knew that much?"

"Being that I'm able to monitor each member of the Circle's personal accounts—"

"You're able to do what?"

"Yeah, you heard me, Raymond. Antonio has given me more than you think and I have been looking at a few things myself, but with that access I was able to see that you've spent right at three hundred thousand dollars since Antonio's incarceration. Silvia's spent—"

Raymond cut her off. "You've been spying on us, Diamond?"

"Call it what you want, nigga. My name is McClendon and now that Antonio is in the background of this shit, I'm making sure I paint this shit with the colors I choose."

Raymond had to laugh. Here he thought Diamond was just some renegade cut to make a fortune with the drugs and resources her brother had. He had no idea she was capable of such actions, and with that realization came the fact that Dell and Silvia knew nothing of Diamond's position among them. She might have been years younger than him, but she was definitely beyond her years when it came to the game she owned. "Stay out of my shit, Diamond."

He could hear her laugh through the phone.

"You're good. You're good, Raymond. I do appreciate all you do for us through and you know that."

"That's what I'm here for," he told her, before ending the call. Knowing the money was spent on something they could flip, he began thinking of the event. His job was to make money for them and that's something he'd continue to do.

***

Chris looked back towards the hallway for any signs of Datrina. He last saw her on the other side of the mansion and was doing his best to avoid her while he discussed things with KP. He'd been called. By the way KP was talking, he knew he couldn't leave the guy with the thoughts he was having. He'd talked him out of the rash decisions he was wanting to make and felt it would be best to at least show KP that not only did he trust him, but he understood where he was coming from. He'd want the same thing for himself had it been Datrina and someone he looked at as a good friend.

"This is what we're going to do, KP." Chris walked to their four-car garage, leaned against the Range Rover he'd been given and told him, "I'm going to take care of Jeff. I'm more than sure Q don't want to see me right now, so you'll—"

"Why you say that?"

Chris looked back towards the door. "I ran into him yesterday and we had a little talk."

"Oh yeah?"

"Listen, nigga. Damn!" Chris didn't have time to get into all that. "You're going to have to get him somewhere remote. The fastest way might be the best way, because you were once friends and when you start thinking about all that and he gets to reminding you of stupid shit, you'll be having second thoughts and—"

"The hell I will."

"You've got to make it look like a robbery at least, KP."

"How about I choke his ass out and make him confess the shit?"

"See, that's what I'm talking about. What the fuck you need a confession for? If you wasn't sure about this shit in the first place, we wouldn't be having this conversation."

"I just want to hear him say it, I guess."

Chris sighed in frustration. "Listen, KP. No confession, no discussion, and no choking. The nigga just might be the one to choke your ass out."

"I'll just shoot him."

"With what?"

"I bought a gun from a guy I know."

"Did you tell him what the gun was for?"

"Nope. I just told him I wanted it."

"As soon as you do it, bring me the gun, KP. Do not go home, do not make any other stops, and do not throw the gun away yourself. Bring it to me."

"You acting like I ain't never stepped on a nigga before."

"Am I?"

"Hell, yeah."

Chris checked his phone to make sure he was on the throw away. He didn't need things coming back to him in any form of fashion. "And, make sure he's dead, KP."

"Don't tell Silvia, Chris. I don't need—"

"Are you serious, Kevin? If that was the case, we'd all be in a meeting somewhere."

"I'm just saying. You know you tell her everything. And, if it ain't her it's Diamond, and you know she tell Silvia every damn thing."

"Just make sure the nigga dead once you do it. And bring me the gun."

"Are you going to kill Jeff?"

Chris closed his eyes. He was hoping like hell this wasn't a mistake and that he didn't have to kill Silvia's husband. "Dead, nigga. Just make sure you kill him."

"When are—"

Chris ended the call, turned and was looking dead at Datrina. "Where you come from?"

"Who were you just talking to, Chris?"

"Huh?"

"You heard me, cross-eyed ass nigga." She reached for his phone.

"Nobody."

"Well, then give me the phone since it was nobody." She held out her hand.

"Datrina, listen. I was just—"

"The phone, nigga, you was just talking to nobody, I got that part."

Chris wasn't the one to keep things from Datrina, and he knew he wouldn't be able to do so now. "I thought you were on the other side of the house?"

"I was until I couldn't find you."

Chris tried walking past her. "What are you looking for me for?"

"The phone, nigga. I'm trying to see who nobody has to make sure is dead." She blocked his exit and gave him a stern look.

"That was KP," Chris exhaled before continuing. "He's going to kill Q."

"What?"

"The nigga acting like he can't live unless he does it so."

"Are you serious? That nigga can't even get rid of a rash, and you're in here encouraging him to kill somebody. Are you serious, Chris?"

He grabbed her before she could make her way back inside. "Datrina, this stays here and the reason I told him that shit is because I know he's not going to do it. The next time we see them niggas they gone be best friend again."

"Have you told Silvia about this?"

"Nobody."

"Oh, him again."Datrina rolled her eyes and said, "If that nigga get caught up, your name is going to be the first thing out of his mouth, and then what?"

"Just trust me on this one, babe. That nigga, KP, ain't built like that and you know it." Chris followed his girl through the hallways and into the walk-in bathroom. He needed to make sure they understood each other.

Datrina faced him and frowned. "Um, don't you have something to do or somewhere to be? Quit following me like I'm about to disappear or something."

"You know I love you, don't you?" Chris grabbed her around her waist and pulled her to him.

"I can tell." She pushed him away and closed the bathroom door. "Just make sure he's dead, Chris. I don't need you getting caught up in that shit."

Chris smiled, nodded and told her, "Let me use your car today?"

"Don't fuck with my shit, nigga. Y'all ain't gonna be squeezing nobody in my shit."

***

Camille pulled into the Denny's eatery and parked two spaces from where Diamond's Corvette sat. They'd spoke briefly over the phone and it was only to agree to the location they'd need for the early breakfast.

Diamond waved Camille over to the corner booth overlooking the parking lot. There were some things she needed her to know and she couldn't wait to tell. "They just refilled the buffet and the breakfast sausages are to die for."

Camille glanced in the direction of the displayed food and decided against it. "I'm good. I'll just find something later."

Once Camille was seated across from her, Diamond took a sip on the fresh juice she drank and told her, "That bitch not even from the states."

"Who?"

"Nava. I stopped by last night acting as if King was cheating on me. I leaned on her shoulder and everything."

"No, you didn't?"

"That stupid bitch was rubbing on my back, talking about I didn't need to be putting up with his shit and that if she was me, she'd leave him and all this other shit. I thought the bitch was going to try to fuck, the way she was all up on me."

"You're scandalous, Diamond."

"The bitch is from Cuba. Got hooked on drugs and partying in high school, and fell for a no-good nigga that had the bitch selling pussy and eventually stripping."

Camille leaned back, chuckled slightly and shook her head. She watched the woman in front of her and the more she listened, the more she was seeing herself in her. The extent a person was willing to go for the people and person they loved had no bounds and was stronger than any other attraction or liking another claimed to have. This was the exact way she was when it came to the men in her life, and it was the only kind of person she'd want either of them with.

"I went along with it when she started talking about wanting to find out if he really was."

"And how is she going to do that?"

"The bitch got to do some digging and before she realizes it, she'll be six feet deep."

Camille eyed Diamond, saw her speak as if it was just another deal or transaction when it came to killing. She looked around them and told her, "I really like you, Chanel."

"I'm baking the bitch a cake as we speak. I'm going to see if I can stuff a surprise in that bitch."

"Whatever you need, just say the word."

"All I need for you to do is stay around King, that way he won't suspect either of us when this shit pop off."

"Will do, Diamond."

Diamond checked the clock on her phone. She was more than sure she'd be receiving a call shortly. After that, the game would begin.

***

Buddy pulled past the security booth, nodded at a couple of guys he'd come to know and lowered his window. "How's it going, guys?"

"We good, Buddy. We haven't seen you in a while. Business slow or what?"

"You can say that." Buddy tossed them an envelope. "Get the kids something nice for the holidays."

He watched them as they tore into the package. This wasn't the first time he blessed their game and with them working security at the waste and disposal site for the City of Dallas, it wouldn't be the last time. Before they could thank him, he pulled off, drove across the scale and headed to his next stop.

CHAPTER SEVENTEEN

Chris thought about ways to approach both Jeff and the situation at hand. He didn't want to come off as a threat to him, but he did want him to know the seriousness of what he'd done and the extent certain people were willing to go to get back what they felt they lost. He parked behind one of the Dually trucks Jeff bought with McClendon money, and climbed out of his Rover. He looked around the neighborhood and was glad he didn't instruct KP to pay the guy a visit.

He knocked three times. "Motherfucker bought the shit they need to," he whispered to himself, noticing the equipment and trucks.

"Can I help you?" Jeff stepped out onto his porch, wearing a frown that told Chris he knew something was wrong.

"Jeff?"

"Yeah, that's me. What's up?"

"Ah, yes, I'm with the McClendon Construction Company and I would like to know if you have a minute." Chris then began digging through the satchel he carried.

"Um, what is this about?"

"I'm just here to inform you of the legalities of what's about to happen."

"Legalities?"

Chris pulled out several sheets of paper he'd drawn up before leaving the house. He told him, "A while back, one of the McClendon employees was robbed at gunpoint and money was taken in the course of it and your name came up and—"

"Whoa! Whoa! Whoa! Gunpoint?"

Chris turned the papers to where Jeff could see them. "It says here that you, along with Quinten Rivers, robbed a Kevin Piersons for over six hundred thousand dollars, and the company has decided to press charges against your person and your company."

"Press charges? Over six hundred thousand dollars? Are you serious?"

"I'm just giving you the heads-up, sir."

"I didn't rob nobody for that money. It was . . ."

Chris smiled in order to cover the laugh he wanted to give. He knew Q and KP dealt with some clowns at the labor pool, but they never mentioned they were taking advantage of their ignorance. "You just might have to do some prison time for this, because they're not about to let up."

"Prison time? Man, I ain't going back to the pen. Is there anyway we can make this shit go away?"

Chris reached into his satchel a second time. "Um . . ."

"Come in." Jeff ushered him inside, offered him a drink and began looking over the papers Chris had.

"Being that the money was to be used to purchase some of the same things you spent it on, I'm more than sure if you just signed it all back over to the McClendon Company and came to work under its umbrella, I could make most of this go away."

"No charges will be filed after that, right?"

Chris shook his head. "I'm more than sure I can talk them out of it."

"And, I come work for McClendon and his company?"

"Her, McClendon is a she."

"Um, where do I sign?"

Chris watched as Jeff signed over everything and anything, to keep from being charged in a robbery he didn't commit. The irony of it all wasn't lost to Chris at all. He'd seen people do the same things many times, knowing it would be just as if they did commit the crime they knew little or nothing about. He was just about to leave when he told Jeff, "We're doing some work at the Irving Plaza and I would like to see you and the crew there as a sign of good faith."

"I'll round up the guys I got and we'll be there. Tell Mrs. McClendon we'll be there."

***

To Kevin Piersons, it was as simple as inviting Q out for a drink, taking him to some low budget motel and leaving him slumped behind one of the dumpsters there. Only thing was that Q kept sending his calls to voicemail and he wasn't at home when KP did arrive. He'd been sitting in Q's driveway all of seven minutes when he got to thinking about how things would be afterwards. He checked his surroundings every so often, as Chris instructed him. Hoping to leave everyone that saw him with the impression that all was well between them, he waved, smiled at the neighbors he knew and even inquired about his friend's whereabouts. He couldn't help but notice how some of the neighbors looked at him as if they knew what he came to do.

KP looked over the gun he'd bought and thought about Chris's instructions to take it directly to him. Just before he was able to put the car in reverse, he spied a cop car turning at the top of the street. He eased the gun between the seat and the console. "Shit!" he muttered, seeing the cop car stop and park at the top of the street. KP then figured one of the neighbors had called them and they were just waiting for him to leave, before hitting the sirens and pulling him over.

He slowly reached for his phone, careful not to make any sudden moves. "Shit." He tried to erase the numbers and the calls that could be used against him. They were on him now. He was praying they couldn't make out the figure sitting behind the tinted windows of the Escalade. KP had to think fast. They were on him and he knew it.

Hoping he was making the right decisions, he put the truck in reverse and pulled out. If they did pull him over and ask questions, he'd just tell the cops that he was just wanting a beer and he came by to see if his friend wanted one also. No, he'd tell them that they had a job to do and that he was there to pick him up. "Yeah. I just swung by to pick him up," he agreed with the thought he was having. KP checked his rear view mirror, then slowly turned at the bottom of the street. He made the block just to make sure they hadn't followed him. "Them hoes probably called ahead on my ass," he told himself, knowing there was no way he'd be able to escape them once they did figure out his agenda. As for now, Q's house was the last place he wanted to be. As soon as he hit the highway, he floored the huge truck. He had to make it to the salon. "Fuck that shit."

***

Diamond was surprised to see Dell had actually shown when he said he would. She'd been expecting his call and some watered-down excuse for not being able to do what she needed done but when seeing the huge smile he displayed, she found herself second-guessing it. She unlocked her passenger side door after seeing him walk around her car.

"I'm glad I was able to catch up with you before you got in traffic," he told her after climbing in.

"What you got for me?" She watched him pull a set of keys from his pocket.

"Two-bedroom town home, twenty minutes from the Three Rivers Facility. Spacious living areas. Fireplace and you even have two parking spaces."

"What's the other key for?"

Dell laughed. "It's for your storage unit that's attached. I know you might need a little more room whenever you do make arrangements."

"Yeah, you're right."

"It's in the rear of the area, just in case you need a little privacy."

Diamond threw the keys in the compartment under her armrest and told him, "It's just until my bro get out of that hell hole."

"Yeah, tell me about it."

"Have you heard anything concerning his case?" She watched him shrug.

"Not since the last time Silvia said something about it."

"Well, I appreciate you, Dell. I really do. Um, I was thinking that we should sit down and put our differences aside, and get with Silvia and Raymond and let them know what's up."

"All right then. Get at me later, Diamond. I have a couple ideas I would love to run by everyone."

"Count me in." Diamond waited until Dell pulled off before calling Camille. Her plans were coming together just the way they discussed and now was not the time for mistakes. Now, all she had to do was make sure King didn't interfere.

Datrina's smile faded the moment KP entered the salon. The look in his eyes told more of the story than he ever would. The way he continued to look back towards the door and the way he checked his phone were the tell-tale signs she used to gauge his quilt. She looked around to see who else might be noticing that KP was tripping and sure enough, Somolia let him have it.

"There they go, KP. There they go!" Somolia laughed, seeing him spin to where she pointed.

"Somolia, you tripping," he told her, still making sure no one was actually walking in behind him.

"You sliding up in here like you running from somebody, what's up?"

"Ain't shit, just chilling."

"Who you running and hiding from, nigga?" Silvia asked, seeing the same thing Somolia was able to point out.

"I'm not running from nobody, what y'all tripping on?"

"You," Silvia told him and went to see outside the salon door.

"Don't go out there!" KP stopped her.

All the women present looked in his direction with questioning glares. KP was known to do some crazy things, but it was now obvious that someone was after him.

"Nigga, if somebody run up in here looking for you, I'm pointing your ass out, KP." Silvia yanked her arm from him and started towards her office.

KP followed.

"Don't be following me," she told him before entering her office and closing the door.

"What you do now, KP?"

KP frowned, looked at each of the women and asked, "What y'all looking at me for? I haven't done shit."

"Well then, why you ain't took your other hand out of the pocket of that hoodie you're wearing?"

"The question is why in the hell you wearing a hoodie in the first place?"

"Is there a law that says no hoodie or something?"

Somolia pointed her comb at him. "I hope you don't plan on robbing us because you'd just be practicing, 'cause we broke as hell up in here."

The other women laughed.

"Ain't nobody trying to rob y'all?"

"Then, what's the gun for, Kevin?"

Datrina closed her eyes. She'd warned Chris against this and now that KP was running around with the gun he used in the murder, she had to say something to get people off the case they were building against him. "You're still thinking a motherfucker trying to steal the damn truck?"

KP faced her and frowned. "What?"

"I heard that someone tried to steal your truck and you finally got some protection." She subtly winked at him.

"Um—"

"You ought to take that truck back to the dealership and ask for that new Prestige alarm," said one of the women that drove a Cadillac herself.

"Prestige? I've got the Excalibur and you ain't taking shit when it comes to them," said another.

Somolia pulled out her key fob and showed them the small light built into it. "If I push this button, my shit starts by itself. If I push the other, it shuts off. The only thing my alarms don't do is drive that motherfucker."

"Hell, if I paid a hundred thousand dollars on a car, mine would do all that and more."

Datrina exhaled, rolled her eyes at KP and told the women, "You take my shit, you might as well call and tell me where you going, because my phone gonna follow your ass anyway."

"Yeah, I need for you to show me how to hook my shit up like that, Datrina."

"Speaking of phone, let me call Chris right quick." She headed outside and KP followed.

***

King was sitting at the table looking over some numbers, when Camille walked up and wrapped her arms around him from behind and kissed his cheek.

"What was that for?"

"I'm just loving on my best friend, is all."

So, why am I feeling that something is about to be said in addition to you loving all on me?" He looked up at her.

"I'm beginning to see that these days are being taken away from me and I'm feeling some type of way, I guess."

"You tripping." King pulled her onto his lap and held her.

"It would seem that way, huh?"

"There are always going to be days like this, Camille. I'm not going anywhere."

"You know, Diamond used to scare me at one time, because I thought she was reckless and rash, and that she didn't really think things through before she did them but she continues to surprise me at every turn."

"What has she done now?"

"It's just me realizing that she is me and I am her."

King kissed her forehead. "She's beginning to weigh on you, ain't she?"

"I wouldn't necessarily say that. She's just shown me that she'll be good for you."

"Oh, really?

"Um-hmm."

King rocked her. "What happened to that 'no woman is good enough for me' speech?"

"I should have said average woman." Camille smiled up at him.

Oh, so now my woman is crazy?"

"She's not average, King, and if you have a department to place her in, then that's on you."

"Since we're talking about crazy, I guess it's to say that she's exactly like you."

"Is that why you love her?" Camille raised herself so she could gauge his answer better, as well as sneak a peek at the clock.

"Nothing and no one will ever replace you, so the answer to that is no. I just saw something different in Diamond. I saw a space I could fill. A space I wanted to fill in her life and I could see her filling that space in my life as well." He looked off in thought before saying, "Love is funny like that."

"What you know about love, Kengyon Johnson?"

"I know that it feels so good to be loved, and just as good to be able to love."

"And, how would you go about showing this love you claim to be able to give?"

"Um, I'd give the world for it and all that I have to keep it."

Camille smiled. "Sounds like something a fool would say."

"And do."

"Well, if you really love her the way you claim, why don't you marry her?"

King looked his friend in her eyes, saw true sincerity and told her, "I've been thinking about just that, but I didn't want her to feel as if it was some rebound marriage or anything."

"She knows better than that, King."

"You think she'll—"

"She'll what?" She wanted for him to say it.

"You know."

"No, I don't know."

King smiled. "Let me think about it."

"Try not to take too long, because guys are lined up at the door trying to get at her."

"What about you, Camille?"

"What about me?"

"When are you going to trade your heels for house shoes and trade in the sports car for mini vans?"

"Find something else to entertain yourself with King, that's not going to happen."

He squeezed his best friend, kissed her forehead and repeated his earlier statement, "Let me think about it."

"If you lose her, King, she's not coming back, so think about that as well."

Camille lost herself in his embrace. She'd thought about that very thing years ago, but wasn't ready to see herself in that light. She loved the game and the things it offered but she loved life more and only recently did she even think about seeing herself under a man and not having to be her own way maker. And, the fact that he was serving a life sentence erased even that.

***

"I wish I would have been here when that bitch showed up all distraught and shit. I would have fucked something," said the gold-toothed guy.

"You should have called us, Nava."

"What I should have done was fuck her myself. If I would have sucked on that dumb bitch's pussy, she would have given me everything." Nava walked from the living area they sat, into the kitchen. She grabbed the saucer from over the vents and cut herself a couple of lines. She'd turned plenty of women out and was more than sure the gullible, fragile woman she had in her grasp the day before was easy pickings. The only reason she didn't was because she needed her now. With King distancing himself from her, she had the next best thing and she wasn't about to mess it off in her attempt to seduce her. After consoling Diamond for right at two hours she gave her something to confide in. She'd become the woman Diamond would come to vent about King and she'd become that friend she needed to uncover King's infidelity, as well as where he kept the torture she was after.

After hearing that King was continually traveling out of town, Nava had a pretty good idea what he was going out of town for and as soon as she found out where she'd played her hand and once the deck was shuffled, she'd be on her way again.

"Come give me some of that pussy before I leave, Nava."

She walked back into the living area, handed the other guy the saucer and told him, "Hit that shit because when I finish fucking him, it's you turn."

Nava stepped out of the panties she was wearing, rubbed a finger full of cocaine on her lips and clit and began sucking her fingers. The party was about to start and money was about to be made. "It can't get no better than this," she told the two of them before laying down and spreading her legs, exposing one of the prettiest pussies they'd ever seen.

CHAPTER EIGHTEEN

Buddy walked four blocks to the would-be salon. There was a feeling he couldn't shake when it came to Somolia's salon being set on fire. He'd heard the reports from different ends and being that he knew the streets in a way many didn't, he went to them for answers. He walked to the corner of the plaza, bought a paper from the stand and looked over the area. Repairs had been done to the salon and it was just weeks away from its grand opening. This time he was going to make sure it happened.

The sight of the huge truck alone caused him to venture to the rear of the buildings, because either someone was moving out or about to move in and at this time of night, it was obvious that whatever was taking place wasn't for all to see. Buddy strolled past the storage facility at the far end of the plaza to where the truck and its occupants had backed in. And, after the rear of the truck was raised, he saw three guys began loading the truck with all types of merchandise and equipment. He was just about to go about his business, until he saw them loading swivel chairs into the truck. The same swivel chairs he'd heard Diamond speak about. He didn't have to see the rest of the things they had to realize whose they were, and therefore didn't need to ask any questions. These guys had taken from his girl and that was something he wasn't going to allow.

After checking the area a second time, he walked to where two of the guys stood. "Asians?" he questioned himself when getting a better look at them. It then made sense to him. The owners of the Asia Islands salon across the street must have felt the soon-to-open salon would be a competition they didn't need and after a second glance, Buddy realized there weren't any other salons in the entire area. "Excuse me," he called out to them.

It was then they finally noticed his presence and it was the advantage Buddy always seemed to find when it came to the work he did. He pulled the MAC-11 from its holster, aimed and squeezed a round of silenced shots into the closest guy and seeing the others freeze in fear, he pointed towards the storage. "What all you guys got in there?" Buddy let off another series of silenced shots, dropping them both. He walked to where he stood over them and fired fatal head shots, just in case. These guys had cost him over a hundred thousand dollars, and owed that in blood. Instead of looking over the stolen merchandise, Buddy walked away, leaving both bodies and swivel chairs in that darkened section of Irving Plaza. He knew the cops would discover the gruesome scene, as well as begin their investigation and when they did, he'd be long gone. This was his game and this was what he was willing to do for his woman, for his Somolia.

***

King watched Camille busy herself in the kitchen. He didn't know what she was up to but the conversation they just had caused him to wonder. He was hoping she wasn't thinking about pulling stakes on him, or trying to get him to do so by pushing Diamond and his decisions to marry her across the table.

Him being with Diamond was definitely in the writing, but he wanted just that for her also. He wanted nothing more than that for his best friend. He grabbed the remote, acted as if he was engrossed in the program and watched her, until his phone distracted him. He saw who the caller was and smiled.

"Hey, babe."

Diamond couldn't help but smile when hearing King's greeting. Regardless of how many times she spoke with him in the course of the day, he always greeted her as if he hadn't seen or heard from her in days. Weeks even. Her brother was also known to do just that. "What are you doing?" she asked in her most seductive tone.

"Waiting on you."

"Really?"

"That and sitting here listening to Camille."

"What's she talking about?" Diamond watched the door to Nava's apartment open and two guys walk out. She watched as she kissed each of them.

"You know how she is when she has nothing to do," he told her.

"You know I'm missing you, right?" Diamond kept her eyes on Nava. Watched her wave the guys off, watched her blow a thick cloud of smoke into the night air. She saw that she was now alone.

"Well then, why can't we be together tonight?"

Diamond chuckled. "Is that what you want?"

"Always."

"You just want to fuck me, King."

"And there's always that when it comes to you, Diamond."

"Umm, tell me what you want to do to me." Diamond closed her eyes, eased down in the seat of her car and raised her left leg. She rubbed herself.

"Now?"

"Yeah, tell me what you want to do to me and how you think it should be done."

"Diamond, you're crazy. You know that?"

"I'm waiting, King."

"Camille is right here, Diamond."

"And?"

"Why don't you just let me come to you and show you?"

Diamond saw the living room light go off in Nava's apartment. She thought about her climbing into a hot bath or a warm bed even. She told him, "Since you're scared to entertain me, I'll just find other ways to entertain myself."

"Don't play with me, Diamond. You know I would if Camille wasn't here."

"I'm just playing with you, babe. Let me finish getting my nails done. This woman already looking at me like I'm crazy as hell," she lied.

"Well, you are."

"For you, I am."

"And for you, I am."

"So, you know what it is tomorrow, right?" Diamond checked herself in the rear view mirror, pulled her hair back in a high ponytail and opened her door. "I'm more than sure you'll remind me when that time comes."

"Just get it ready. Take you a couple of them blue pills and put some Orajel on that tongue."

"You're a freak, Diamond."

"Tomorrow, I'll be whatever you want me to be, but right now I have to go."

"Tomorrow it is, then."

Diamond climbed out of the car and headed for Nava's. She was definitely looking forward to tomorrow.

Nava straightened her place to where no signs of her sexcapade were evident. She was feeling herself in the worst way and after the sex they just had, a nice hot bath and some sleep was all she needed. Hearing her doorbell chime, the thought of doing that took a back seat. "Who the hell is this?" she asked no one in particular. Seeing Diamond through the peep hole, she hurried to open the door. "Diamond?"

"I got it."

Nava pulled Diamond inside, checked to make sure she wasn't being followed and closed the door, as if her best interest was at heart. "You got what?"

"A copy of the key and the address to his other spot he's sharing with some other woman." Diamond handed her the keys Dell gave her.

"Come in here," Nave led Diamond into her living area and once they were seated, she looked over the keys. "How'd you get these?"

"I drove his truck earlier and went to get a copy made."

"We got his ass, Diamond." Nava clenched the keys in her hand and smiled. This was happening. Finally. "Now, we just need to bust his ass. I'm going to drive over there myself."

"It's in San Antonio. This is the place he goes to every week."

"San Antonio?"

"Yep."

"And you have the address?"

Diamond showed her the address on her phone. "Here it is right here."

"When do you think is the best time to go there?"

Diamond looked her dead on, needing her to think what she was about to tell was confidential. "He said something about needing to sort out a drop this weekend."

"A drop?"

"That's what I heard him say while he was on the phone."

"You think he's giving her money?"

Diamond watched the way Nava leaned closer towards her. She grabbed her hand and placed it on her lap. "I'm not sure. He did take a large sum of money there a couple of days ago and after I asked him about it, he just said he didn't feel safe with it in his place."

"Yeah?"

"Do you think he's playing me with some other woman?"

"I used to say the same thing about that bitch, Camille. She—"

"I can't stand that bitch." Diamond closed her eyes to add effect, squeezed Nava's hand and pushed herself back into the sofa. "That bitch always trying to keep us apart."

"She did the same shit when me and King were together." Nava shook her head.

"I wish it was a way to get her out of the way."

"You know what, Diamond? Fuck that bitch and whoever this other bitch is. You need to hit his ass where it hurts and I'm going to help you."

"How?" Diamond watched her with pleading eyes.

"His money. We're going to wait until he does another drop and then we're going to hit this address, 'cause I'm positive this is where he's keeping it."

"I don't—"

"'Listen to me, Diamond, he's not even going to suspect you 'cause you'll be with him when I go there to get it. Then, I'm going to come back here and we're going to act like nothing ever happened. By the time he realizes his money is gone, he's going to regret fucking over us—I mean you. He's going to think that bitch took it."

"You sure?"

Nava pulled at Diamond's ponytail until her head tilted. She gently kissed her neck. Stuck her tongue into her ear and told her, "This is what I do."

Diamond leaned back and closed her eyes. "I—"

"Shh," Nava coaxed her. "I'll give you what you need, Diamond. I got what you want."

Diamond tensed when feeling Nava squeeze her thigh. "I'll give you money."

"Don't worry about money. Don't worry about nothing. You let me handle this shit,"

"Have you ever done anything like this before, Nava?'

"Done what? Kissed a girl?"

"Yeah."

"I turn bitches out, Diamond. I'm that bitch hoes can't get enough of."

Diamond laughed. Feeling the warmth of Nava's hand covering her pussy, she grabbed her wrist and eased it away. "Let this be your reward when it's done."

Nava bit her lip, looked Diamond in her eyes and told her, "I've been wanting to fuck your pretty ass and as soon as this is over, I'm going to blow your mind."

"You think so?"

"I know so."

***

KP smiled once they were outside. He was thankful for Datrina and she needed to know it. "Thanks."

"I don't what you smiling at me for. You and Chris ain't going to be worrying me with this shit y'all about here doing."

"I feel you. Believe me, I'm not doing shit."

"You shouldn't be."

It must have been the way she spoke the words, along with the way she looked at him, 'cause KP felt there was something he needed to explain. "I'm for real. I didn't do shit."

"Of course you didn't."

KP looked back toward the doors of the shop to make sure they were still alone. He told her, "I'm serious, Datrina, I didn't do it. I didn't."

"That's what you need to stick to then, KP, 'cause if this shit falls back on Chris, we're going to have a problem."

"There's nothing to worry about because I didn't do nothing."

"So, who were you supposed to kill, KP?"

"Nobody."

"Ahh, nobody huh?"Datrina shook her head. "Well, I'm not going to play this little game with y'all, but just know this, if I'm ever questioned about this nobody person, I'm pointing your ass out."

"You tripping."

"And put that damn gun up."

"Chris told me to bring it straight to him after I—"

"And what the hell is he going to do with it that you can't?" Datrina threw a hand on her hip and watched him.

"He told me to bring it to him and that's what I'm doing."

"I thought you didn't do anything with it?"

"I didn't."

"Then, what does he need it for?"

"That's what he told me to do if I did do something."

"Why didn't you?" Datrina knew how to pick KP and the longer she got him to talk, the more she understood.

" 'Cause he wasn't there?"

"You were supposed to make sure he was dead, KP."

"I know. But when I went by his house, he wasn't there and the cops pulled on his street, then I froze up."

"Whose street?"

"Q's street."

"And what the hell you doing on Q's street, KP?"

"That's who I was going to kill. I—" KP stopped, closed his eyes and lowered his head.

"What the hell you kill Q for, KP? Are you serious?"

"I didn't kill him. Datrina."

"So, Chris did instead?"

"Hell naw. He just—"

Datrina threw her hands up as if it was none of her business and he was thankful for it, because he'd already said too much. "Let me see what ya friend got going on right quick. I'm beginning to see that lying has become a characteristic both of you share."

***

Chris turned at the top of the street and slowly pulled off. He had a feeling KP wouldn't be able to do what needed to be done and came to see for himself. The only thing he didn't like about the picture he was seeing was that there were no lights on in Q's house. He awaited KP's call so he could discard the weapon used, but seeing his girlfriend's number instead, he knew she'd picked him. "What he say, Datrina?"

"Once this nigga get to talking, all kinds of shit pour out."

"Where is he now?"

"Standing right here looking like I got some handcuffs or something."

"Put him on."

KP frowned. "You already knew?" He grabbed his phone from Datrina. "Yeah, what's up?"

"Is it done?"

"Naw, I froze up."

"Well then, chill out. You're good."

"What do you want me to do with this gun?"

"Do you have it on you now?"

"Yeah, his dumb ass brought it into the salon," Datrina yelled from over his shoulder.

"Yeah," KP held his finger to his lips.

"Just put the damn gun back in the truck, KP."

"What about the cops?"

"KP, put the damn gun in the truck. I'm on my way there now."

After handing Datrina her phone and hurrying to return the gun, he walked back into the Totally Awesome Salon. Datrina followed him.

***

Somolia answered her phone on the second ring. "Hey love."

"You busy?"

"Not now," she lied. There was no way she was about to let him end their call that fast. She hadn't heard from Buddy in days and wanted to thank him for the money he gave to help rebuild her salon.

"I'm missing you."

"Come show me." Somolia walked around her station and sat in the empty chair at Datrina's station.

"I would love that. But, first, I would like to know what I need to come and show."

"How about you show me how to come?" Somolia smiled at the women that were now giving her their undivided attention. She snapped her fingers, silencing them. She pressed speaker.

"How about I tell you where I want you to come?"

With everyone listening to Somolia and what she had going on, Datrina and KP felt safe. She and KP didn't have to explain the nature of their secret meeting. For that, they were both grateful.

Nicole Goosby

CHAPTER NINETEEN

With Somolia and Datrina gearing up for the grand opening, Silvia was left to opening the salon until she could get some of the other women in the routine. It had been a while since she owned the chore. She had to call Somolia just to be reminded that the security code had been changed back to its previous setting. Something they had done every ninety days. She'd been there for an hour already and still hadn't opened by the time other beauticians began to show.

Datrina walked in behind a couple of the other beauticians and fell right in sync with their day to day activities. "Silvia, hit the breaker while you're back there."

"Hey, y'all!" Somolia made her presence known as soon as she walked into the building.

"Somolia, there's been like ten people calling for you in the last five minutes."

Silvia came from back and hugged the women.

"I hope they ain't no bill collectors, because I'm not in the mood today."

Somolia checked her phone, sat in on its charger and walked behind the front desk.

"Girl, you can't be skipping out on your bills when you open up shop. I don't need motherfuckers coming here looking to get paid, just because you ain't doing what you're supposed to be doing." Somolia looked from Silvia to Datrina then back to Silvia, who was walking back into her office.

"Is KP here?" Somolia said, loud enough for him to hear.

She and Datrina watched KP step out of Silvia's office.

He yawned.

"I know this bitch ain't been up in here fucking." Somolia rolled her eyes.

"No, Somolia, I just happened to be the one that drove her to work, if that's okay with you." KP walked to where Datrina stood and hugged her.

"Sound like some jealous shit to me," Datrina laughed and seeing Somolia eye him, she laughed even harder.

"Jealous? Please. The dick I'm sucking and fucking is much longer and a hell of a lot stronger." Somolia snapped her fingers above her head.

Silvia spoke there and then. "And, I hope like hell it's enough for you, because the next time you and KP trip out—"

"They're not," Datrina cut in, knowing if things went unchecked, it would be the topic of conversation for the rest of the day.

"Girl, please, you can have that dick. I've moved on." Somolia winked at KP, knowing it would be something someone responded to.

"All right, Somolia."

"You know I was just fucking with you, Silvia. KP know better than to wave that motherfucker in my face. Don't you, Kevin?"

Datrina pointed a mirror at KP. "Don't say shit, nigga."

KP threw his hands up and made his way to the back. Today, he was going to chill with his wife.

"So, what happened last night, bitch?" Datrina knew Somolia was dying to be asked and seeing her climb into the empty chair, she only smiled.

"I had to swallow a little something, that's all."

"Your fat ass always swallow, Somolia. That ain't nothing new."

Silvia walked out of her office, greeted a few of the women that entered and took a seat also. She was sure Somolia had a story to tell.

"Yeah, but this time I let him fuck me in my ass first." Somolia smiled.

Datrina, Silvia and the rest of the women present frowned and while a few of them were hoping Somolia was lying, Datrina and Silvia knew better.

"Nasty bitch." Silvia shook her head.

"That don't make any sense, Somolia, and you know it."

Another of the beauticians spoke up in Somolia's defense. "As long as they cleaned that motherfucker first, it's good game."

KP listened from the doorway and hearing of the things Somolia did, he couldn't help but think about the guy she was doing it for. "Lucky-ass nigga."

***

Chris followed Diamond from her bedroom down spiral stairs and into the kitchen. She'd been out of pocket for most of the day and he wanted to know more than she was telling him. If anyone knew Chanel McClendon, it was him and he knew when she was keeping things from him.

"Am I under arrest or something?" Diamond stopped and turned to face him.

"Should you be? I mean, I asked you a simple question and you catch out like I'm the laws or something."

"You asking all these police-ass questions, nigga. I don't have time for that shit."

"So, then just tell me where you were yesterday." He grabbeda bottled water from the fridge and followed her through the hallway.

"I had to go see the pussy doctor, nigga. Damn." Diamond rolled her eyes, stopped at the doors of the theater room and started walking back the other way.

"I bet you did with your freaky ass. You can't be squirting all that sugary shit up in there, Diamond. It'll only give you an infection."

"Really?"

"I'm telling you."

Diamond faced him. "Nigga, you ain't been fucking nobody but Datrina, so you have to be talking about her."

"Matter's not who I'm talking about. Right now, I'm talking to you."

"Well, that ain't what I had to go for."

"You're pregnant?"

191

Diamond laughed.

"Diamond, you pregnant by that nigga?"

She stopped and faced her friend. Diamond smiled. "You know how you sound right now?"

"Are you?"

"No, Chris. I'm not pregnant by him."

Chris's brows raised. "By who then?"

"You nigga.A bitch pregnant by you, motherfucker." Diamond pushed past him.

"Stop lying all the damn time, Diamond. I'm serious."

"Well, stop asking all these police-ass questions. I had to make a couple of runs yesterday. Me and Camille."

"Camille?

"We went shopping."

"Oh yeah?"

"Yep."

"Where are the clothes and shit then?"

"In my ass, nigga. Now leave me alone." Diamond grabbed the first set of keys she could and headed for the garage.

"She ain't gay is she, Diamond?"

"Hell naw."

" 'Cause every time I look up with her and—"

"Chris, I got this end. Please."

"I know you're up to something, Diamond, and I just want you to be careful. Is there something wrong with that?"

Diamond hit the remote, raising the huge door to their garage and walked over to her brother's '68 Camaro. "The questions stop right here. When we get in this bitch, we dropping the top and we gonna ride. Okay?"

Chris acted as if he was zipping side, his lips and throwing away the key. He climbed into the passenger's side, watched her walk around and climb in also. He had questions and once they were on their way, he'd ask them but for now, he needed his friend's approval. They sped past the security booth, turned onto the on-ramp and before she could floor the classic car, he asked her, "Do you think I ought to marry Datrina?"

"You should have married her by now."

"Let's have a joint wedding."

"What?"

"You and King, and me and Datrina. Let's do this shit together."

Diamond faced him and smiled. "You serious, huh?"

"Why not?"

"Nigga, I ain't said shit about getting married. And, I'm not pregnant, Chris, so stop tripping."

"You're my girl, Diamond. You know that, right?"

"It's mutual." Diamond weaved through traffic, found an open lane and floored the Camaro.

Chris checked the resistance of his seat belt and said, "I can't let nothing happen to you, Diamond, so whatever you're out here doing, just be careful."

She smiled before nodding. "I got it, bro. I got it."

"And, slow your ass down. Where are we going anyway?"

"We're riding, remember?"

"Yeah, well, slow this motherfucker down before the wheel come off or something."

"I'm baking a cake, Chris, and I don't need you anywhere around when it blows up." Diamond spoke the words, hoping Chris would let it go. It was now she needed him to understand and respect the call she was making. And he did.

"Just be careful, sis. Just be careful."

***

Camille walked from the window overlooking the lot of her studio apartment. She'd been thinking of both King and Buddy and the fact that they now had women in their lives. Women that were taking more than their time. She was always the one to encourage them when it came to the game they played and the money they made. Now that they'd climbed to elite levels and unexpected heights, she never thought they'd be doing anything different. It wasn't that she didn't want happiness for the two men in her life. But, for her, that was something she was yet to find herself, and therefore didn't think existed. She saw the way they looked at the women they now had. She knew personally the extent they were willing to go also and as bad as she wanted to keep them to herself, she knew that time was ending.

For them to play the game forever was what she wanted, but was something she knew they couldn't do. They'd been more than lucky. That wasn't something to take advantage of or fail to realize. She looked at all she owned and thought of all the things she should have owned, the investments she should have made and the security she should have placed around herself. She thought about Diamond and the fact that she hadn't been in the game as long as she had. But, one thing she knew about Chanel was that she could step away from it all and not miss any of it. The investments she spoke of, the dollars her brother put into her and the things she found interest in, were the things Camille failed to do when it came to her and the circle she was in. She'd been running things for so long that both time and opportunity flew by, and now that she was forced to sit back and look at the game she played, Camille realized it was all for the thrill, the edge of it all. The adrenaline ran through her body when the speedometers climbed past life-threatening speeds. The power she felt when the counters beeped and hundreds of thousands had been made and the thrill of knowing that whatever happened, her guys would be there.

It was now she realized she had to be there for them in other ways. It was nothing for her to count out a couple of million dollars cash but when looking at what she had to show for it, when looking at the security she should have placed around her and her team, she saw nothing. All she owned was a couple of high-end sports cars, a studio apartment and the house her brother Terry lived in and used as a safe to keep the millions of dollars they'd made over the years. Without the game, she had nothing, and that's what she was about to change.

She walked over to where Buddy sat and smiled down at him. "You know what, Buddy?"

"What's up?"

"We need to invest in something."

"Why haven't we?"

She sat beside him, leaned over to where her shoulders pressed into his and told him, "Got comfortable, I guess."

"That's what me and King offer you."

"Yeah, and now that the two of you are leaving me, I have to start thinking of things I didn't normally have to."

"I'm not going anywhere, Boss Lady. I've saved more money than I would have without you. Because of you, I'm able to drop a couple hundred thousand and not miss it."

"Saved money don't make money, Buddy. We had to invest it in areas to where we'll see favorable returns. It takes money to make money."

"Then, let's invest it."

Camille raised slightly, wanting to see what the big guy had to play with. "How much you got?"

"I got a million for you."

"A million?"

"That and some, but for the most part, that's what I'm willing to play with."

"Damn, I didn't know we'd been playing that long."

"Over five years and some."

Camille stood. "Then, it's settled. I'll put up a million also and with King's million, we'll become players of a different game and hopefully, a more lucrative one."

***

Somolia had one client under the dryer and another over the basin they used to wash hair. Today was a good day for her and the rest of the women that worked there. There were those new beauticians Datrina interviewed and the others sought after because of the work. This alone was the reason the waiting area was filled with both women and men.

"KP, can you get me another set of rollers from the closet?" Somolia waved at him from where she stood.

It was always that way when he came by the salon. He would be used for something or needed in some way or another. He sighed, turned on his heels and disappeared. "Yeah, I got it."

"Work his ass, girl."

"I'm going to need someone like KP around when I do open up, because ain't nothing like some good hands," said Somolia.

Silvia just looked at her.

"Well, you might as well find someone else, Somolia, because KP ain't going to be the one," Datrina informed her.

"I didn't say shit about KP. I'm just talking in general."

"You're going to need a runner, huh?" asked one of the men sitting in the waiting area.

Somolia looked towards him and nodded, "Yep."

"What you paying?"

Datrina chimed in, "You sound like you're interested."

"I might be if the price is right."

"I'll pay you two-fifty a week, because I'll most likely just need you around on the weekends."

"That's it?"

Somolia stopped and tsked. "Motherfucker, you act like I'm asking you to fluff niggas or something, with your dick-sucking ass. I"

"Somolia!"Datrina called out to her. "You don't even know that man."

The guy stood, snapped his fingers over his head and told Somolia, "Whatever, bitch. One thing I'm not is cheap though."

"Ass hole probably black as hell too," Somolia added, still not letting up. "Bleach, bitch."

Somolia laughed, as did the rest of the women in the salon. She was just about to yell for KP, when the doors opened and two uniformed cops entered. She watched both of them with questioning expressions, hoping they had some good news for her concerning her salon.

"Mrs. Somolia Rhodes?"

"Um, yeah, that's me," she answered and walked to where they stood. "What's up?"

The light-skinned cop pulled out a notepad and asked, "Can we ask you a couple of questions in relation to the fire that happened to your salon?"

"Yeah, go ahead."

"Um, where were you last night between the hours of nine pm and one am?"

Somolia looked towards Datrina. She told the cop, "We were here late last night, trying to get ahead for today. Why? Is there something wrong?"

"You can verify that with the surveillance we have here at the salon," Silvia added.

"Well, there was a shooting and we believe it was done in retaliation to what was done to your salon."

"What does my salon have to with a shooting?"

"The property you listed as stolen was found at the scene of the crime along with members of the Asian syndicate."

"Then why aren't you questioning them instead of her?" Silvia asked.

"They all died from gunshot wounds, ma'am." The other cop looked around at the rest of the clients and beauticians.

"Dead?" Datrina spoke the words that came to her mind. "Oh my God!"

The sound of cosmetic wrappers and rollers caught everyone's attention and when taking notice, they saw KP was scrambling to regain his footing. He was coming from the back with the supplies Somolia requested and a few more items they were sure to need when he saw the cops standing inside the salon. In his attempt to hide, he accidentally knocked over two display shelves and dropped the things he was holding. They'd come for him and he knew it.

"We were all here last night and we don't know anything about a shooting."

"You mind if we took a look at that footage?" the light skinned cop asked.

"Sure." Silvia turned, frowned at he husband and stepped over him and the items he'd spilled.

The cops followed, stepping past KP as they did.

Datrina watched Somolia follow the cops to Silvia's office. She hurried to where KP knelt and whispered, "What the hell is wrong with you?"

"I thought they were here for me."

"I thought you said you didn't do shit?"

"I didn't."

"Then what you tripping on, nigga?"

Datrina helped him with the mess he'd made, all the while praying that Chris wasn't about to be caught up in the murders the cops were now investigating.

Nava had put together the perfect lick. Now that things were coming together for her, she needed to celebrate. She had one of the guys buy an ounce of cocaine and she made sure they kept a nice supply of the mango Kush she liked. "I'm telling y'all, this is it." Nava bobbed to the heavy baseline that blasted through the speakers of the Gentlemen's Club. They filled the corner booth with both drugs and half naked women and she was feeling herself in the worst way.

" I sure hope so cause I'm ready to hit the A.T.L."

"By the time this shit is done and we split the shit up, we'll be on our way to the Islands, nigga. Fuck these states. Nava cut a line of the purest cocaine she'd had since she'd stayed in Cuba.

"We might need to burn this bitch Diamond too."

"Naw, she ain't got shit but what King give her," Nava told them.

"Ain't she the one that gave you this shit," the gold-toothed guy asked after blowing a line himself.

"Yeah, the stupid bitch stole it from King, I'm sure."

"I still wish you would have let me fuck her. It's time for something new."

"Then I suggest you lick out one of these young hoes and do what you do. I'm the only one going to fuck Diamond." Nava handed him a rolled bill and reached for the Ace of Spades bottle sitting on ice. In a couple of days, they'd be swimming in money and despite the possible consequence of coming back to Dallas, she was coming for Diamond. Turning her out would definitely be that reward worth returning for.

Nicole Goosby

CHAPTER TWENTY

With the grand opening just days away, Somolia was feeling the pressure of upholding and maintaining the perfect work place for both herself and the women she'd be employing. The screenings had been done and the selections had been made. With more submissions than either of them had expected, Somolia didn't want to turn anyone down and that was the nature of the meeting they were having this morning.

"I mean, what can you do about it, Somolia? You only have so many stations and booths in that one building." Datrina felt her friend was making a bigger issue out of nothing.

"I know. I just hate turning people around, I guess." Somolia stood, walked to where she was looking out into the lot of the salon and rubbed her temples.

"The way things are going, we're going to have to open up more salons sooner than expected," Chris told the group.

"Who is 'we'?" Datrina asked, knowing he was referring to her running a salon of her own.

"I'm just saying," Chris added.

"Well, don't, because I already told y'all I'm not about to stress myself out trying to run no damn salon." Datrina stood and walked out onto the salon floor.

"Hell, all the shit that comes with opening one can break a bitch. I mean, a fire, a shooting, hiring motherfuckers, firing, murder."

"Don't even remind me, Somolia." Silvia shook her head. It was almost the same way when they opened the first salon. There was a huge fallout about both locations and who they'd employ. But, it just so happened, Silvia's outlook prevailed, and the salon had been running and growing at alarming speeds. It had been many times Silvia wanted to close the doors of her dreams, but because of Antonio and the rest of The Circle, she had to continue to provide an outlet to clean their money until other investments could be made. "It'll all pan out, girl."

"I sure hope so, because I can't deal with all this police stuff every day."

"Then, you need to keep your nose clean and your business straight."

"I'm going to need some help, y'all. I can't do this shit by myself." Somolia lowered her head.

"Listen to me, Somolia, we got you." Chris walked to where she was and wrapped his arms around her.

She fell into his embrace.

"Aw, shit," Silvia began, "She'll be sucking your dick next, nigga."

"Leave the woman alone, Silvia. She's for real."

"I am too."

Somolia shot Silvia a middle finger and told her, "Been there, done that."

"I'll bet you have. And Chris, you standing over there rubbing all on her like she just found out she's got cancer or something"

"Don't even play like that, Silvia. He's just being consoling right now."

Somolia looked up at him and smiled.

"Datrina, come see Chris and Somolia up in here tripping!" Silvia laughed.

"It's always that we want independence in some form or another, but as soon as opposition finds us, we're discouraged and at times we give up on ourselves. You just have to push through this shit, Somolia." Chris tried to break their embrace, but Somolia began squeezing him. She knew Datrina would come running.

"What are they—" Datrina stopped at the doorway and looked at both of them. Saw Chris trying to free himself and Somolia's smile.

"I told you." Silvia laughed at the scene before here.

"Well, at least his dick ain't hard," Datrina told them.

"Just give it a minute, honey. Just give it a minute."

Silvia looked towards her office door just as KP walked by. He'd been busying himself with the needs of all the women that worked there and it was starting to be something all of them noticed. "What's up with KP?" she asked Chris, knowing it would be something he was behind in more ways than they'd let on.

"The hell if I know."

"Have you threatened him lately?"

"Nope. I think he's ready to get things up and running. He's been working non-stop on this project."

"Has Diamond threatened him?"

"No, Silvia, the man has his own mind and is doing what he wants to do."

"Well, call it what you will, but I know somethings bothering him. The way he was acting the other day while the cops were here, you would have sworn he had something to do with that shooting." Silvia watched the way Chris acted as if it was nothing and the way Datrina stole glance in his direction. If there was a sign to read, Silvia was definitely the one to read it and if there was a secret to keep, she was the one to respect it.

"Well, let me get back out here and make this money." Datrina turned.

"The first couple of weeks, it's going to be you and me, Datrina!" Somolia called out to her.

"Whatever, tramp."

Silvia stood, walked to where Somolia and Chris stood and hugged her as well, "I'm going to be so damn happy when your fat ass is gone. I—"

"Your ass going to be sick when you walk up in this bitch and realize I'm gone." Somolia squeezed her friend. This would be a new chapter for her. For them both.

***

Raymond stood when seeing his friend walk through the doors of the visitation room. He could tell Antonio was in good spirits and was hoping it was because of the news he had. Because, he did have some.

"What's good, Raymond?"

Raymond extended his hand before they hugged. "I'm good, man. I'm good."

"How's everything going out there?" Antonio sat, looked toward the vending area and smiled at his friend.

"Better." Raymond was never the one to prolong the inevitable. Now that they were face-to-face, it was time to tell all he'd been up to. "I was about to sell a few of those properties Dell purchased, but the one I wanted to speak to you about was the home he's now living in. It was purchased with McClendon money and was listed as a property for sale, but by the way Dell is living in it, I doubt that's going to happen."

"Don't worry about Dell right now. I just want you to continue doing what you've been doing."

"That's four million dollars, Antonio."

"Don't sweat it. I'm more than sure we can flip it when the time is right."

"Are you sure?" Raymond was hoping for another answer and was looking forward to serving Dell with the eviction notice.

"Positive."

"There are other properties I would like to renovate and make them into plazas. And now that the construction company is in full swing, we have a leg up on that end as well."

"KP finally came around?"

"More like Diamond and Chris convinced him somehow."

They both laughed.

"The woman on some more shit now, Antonio."

"Yeah, so I've heard."

"And, she has Dell playing by a different tune. And, to be honest with you, man, she's got things moving nicely."

"Oh, yeah?"

Raymond smiled and said, "But, I think you know that already. Matter of fact, this was your plan all along, wasn't it?"

Antonio closed his eye and leaned back. He told him, "I'll be home soon, Raymond, and—"

"Yeah, what they talking about?" Raymond watched his friend, hoping there was more, more than what was hoped and wished.

"Just say they found some new evidence."

"What do you need me to do? You need money or what? I'll make sure—"

"I got it, Raymond. Everything's been taken of, homie. You just make sure this stays between the two of us. Okay?"

"Yeah...yeah, you haven't told me anything."

"I need you to make bigger and better investments, because I'm through with the drugs, man. There's too many ways to make a living out there and now that I know better, I have to do better."

"Yeah, I feel ya. I think they'll love that very much."

"By that, you mean, Diamond?"

"Silvia, too. She's looking forward to the day all of us do."

"Speaking of Silvia, you and her still—"

"Naw, she's really trying to make it work with KP."

"Yeah?"

"And, I have to respect that."

Antonio watched him. He knew better. "Sounds good, but we both know better than some shit like that. You've been chasing that woman for years and I doubt very seriously you throwing in the towel now."

"You were always the one that wanted us together, but—"

"Hell, every time I turned around, the two of you were getting caught doing something."

"Then came Dell."

"And Somolia," Antonio added.

"And Somolia."

Both of them shared a laugh, talked about business, relationships and Diamond. They always talked about Diamond.

***

Chris was sitting, listening to both Somolia and Silvia when his phone rang. He'd been expecting Diamond's call for the past few hours and seeing a number other than hers displayed on his phone, he answered it with a question.

"What's up?"

"Chris?"

"Yeah, what's up?" Chris frowned, looked in Silvia's direction and stood. "Is Diamond with you? I've been trying to contact her for the longest and haven't been able to reach her."

"Oh, um, she went to see her brother today and she most likely has her phone off." Chris shrugged when seeing Silvia give him a dubious expression. He'd spoken to her earlier and didn't know why she just didn't tell King that she was to visit her brother that morning, but whatever the case, he was going to cover for her as best he could.

"Oh, ok. Um, if you hear from her before I do, let her know that I've . . ."

Silvia didn't know what the play was but she told Chris, "Raymond went to see Antonio today."

"Hello?" King asked, hearing the woman's voice in the background.

"Yeah, King. I'm still here."

"Who was that?"

"That was Silvia and I'm more than sure Diamond went to visit her brother."

"But, she told me she had something to do with you this morning."

Chris could tell from the pitch in King's voice that he was worrying about something and now that Silvia told both of them something different from what Diamond told them, he began to wonder and worry as well. "Let me see if I can get through to her, King. I'll get back at you in a few."

"Get at me, Chris."

Datrina walked in at the close of the conversation and when hearing Diamond's name, she told them, "Diamond stopped by the house earlier this morning. She wanted my other phone."

"For what?" Silvia asked, not being about to make sense of the fact Diamond had lied to everyone about where she was.

"She wanted to track the car she gave that girl."

"For what?" Chris frowned."

"The hell if I know." Datrina shrugged.

"Shit."

"What's going on, Chris?" Silvia asked before rubbing her own temples.

Chris thought about the conversation he and Diamond had. He thought about her plea for him to trust her, for him to let her handle that matter and that she didn't want them anywhere near what she had going on. He told her, "She said she was making a cake, so I guess we'll find out soon enough." Chris exhaled, walked over to the window and lost himself in the thoughts he was having. He whispered, "Be careful, Diamond."

Camille grabbed King's phone and sat in on the counter. He'd been looking at its screen ever since he hung up with Chris and it was getting to her. She'd seen him obsess over Diamond before but because he couldn't reach her now, he was a wreck and she hated seeing him like this. "She's probably out trying to surprise you or something, King. Let the woman have her space."

"I do, I am, Camille, but it's not like her to just not be reachable."

"King, will you sit down, please? The woman will call you as soon as she can. You act as if she's just up and left or something. Are you even listening to yourself, King, how can she be denied wanting to see her own brother?"

"Something's not right, Camille. I can't put a finger on it, but I just know something's not right?"

Camille watched him pace her living area. It was killing her not being able to tell what she knew. With all King had going on, she was really hoping Diamond knew what she was doing. She needed for Diamond to come out on top and that was something she had to keep to herself.

For reasons he didn't know, King grabbed his phone and called Nava. He hadn't heard from her in days and was hoping she didn't have anything to do with Diamond's sudden disappearance. He'd specifically told her to not go anywhere near Diamond and now that she couldn't be reached or found, he was praying his demands hadn't gone unheard. "She's not answering either." He looked back at Camille.

"Who's not answering, King?'

"Nava."

"And what does she have to do with Diamond not wanting to be bothered?" Camille threw her hands up as if him relating the two made no sense.

"I don't know, but we're about to find out." He nodded at Buddy. "Ride with me right quick."

Before she could either protest or deter their actions, they were out of the door.

"King!"

"We'll hit you in a few, Camille. I have to find Diamond."

She could only watch as King and Buddy squeeze into her Audi and speed off. There was nothing she could do for either of them, and she was now hoping she didn't have to.

King pushed Camille's Audi as hard as he could. He raced past police cruisers, semi's and everything else keeping him from his Diamond. For either of them to not be reachable was beyond him and with the feeling he was now having something had to give. He immediately thought about the gold-toothed guy and the other man he saw when Nava first came back. Them possibly hurting Diamond as some kind of retaliation crossed his mind and when seeing it visually, he asked Buddy, "You strapped?"

"Always."

"It's not like her to be out of pocket this long and with Nava not answering, I—" King could fathom it.

"We'll find 'em, King."

King nodded, hit the exit ramp and made his way to Nava's. He had to be sure and this was the only way for him to be.

Diamond ignored the calls as long as she could before shutting her phone off and placing it face down in the passenger's seat of the Camaro. The only thing of importance to her at the moment was the tracker phone she'd gotten from Datrina. She'd called Nava earlier that morning, after making another call to inform her that King had just returned from delivering a package. After getting the tracker phone from Datrina, she hit the highway as well. It took her all but twenty minutes before spotting the Pontiac convertible she'd given Nava, as well as the black Town Car that followed her. Diamond checked the modified Glock Chris bought for her to make sure the slide worked and that it was fully loaded. This would be the day and if everything worked the way she wanted, she'd be back in Fort Worth before anybody knew any better.

With Nava in sight, she trailed them eight cars back and while knowing where she was heading, she sat back and drove. The police scanner continually alerted her as to where they were and with this knowledge, she was more than ready...

King pulled into the Broad Moore apartment complex and drove straight to the back. He looked for Nava's convertible before parking in the first space he came upon. Instead of knocking on the front door, he told Buddy, "I'm going around to the back." King jumped the wooden fence and was relieved to find the patio door unlocked. "Nava!"

Nothing.

"Nava!" King stepped inside, only to find himself alone. He ran to the back rooms. Nothing. It wasn't until he was able to look past her closet doors that he realized all of Nava's clothes were gone. The bed was still there, the furnishings were there, but no sign of Nava. "Shit."

King walked out of the front door, saw Buddy standing there and told him, "She's gone."

Buddy stepped past King, his hand still in the jacket he wore. He walked the living area to see if there were any signs of a struggle. Any signs of blood. Nothing. He pointed.

King walked into the kitchen and picked up the folded piece of paper. It was Nava's handwriting.

King,

If you're reading this, it means you did stop by to check on me. LOL. I've been doing a lot of thinking and had to realize that things weren't the same between us. The things you said as well as the things you do, showed me that there was no love lost and that you really do love her. I want nothing but the best for you, Kengyon, and always have. With that being said, I'm moving on. I'm not going to be the one to step on your happiness with my baggage. (SMILE). So, I'm headed home to rebuild my life. I appreciate all you did for me while I was there. It meant a lot.

As for your new woman, I don't trust her, King. There's just something about the way she looks at you that I can't see past, so just be careful with her. Something tells me she's not who she claims to be. Anyways, she's your only problem now. Please don't look for me, King. Don't make this harder than it is for me. I'll always love you. But, you already know that.

Forever yours,
La'Navia Munez

King handed the folded piece of paper to Buddy. "She's gone." As bad as he wanted to see Nava get herself together, he knew that wasn't likely but now that she'd decided to move on, he was going to respect it. Reading those words allayed his anxiety slightly, but with Diamond still out there, he still worried. The thing he was sure of this time was that Camille had nothing to do with the decision Nava made. Unlike the last time, there was no money missing. Nava even left the furniture he bought for her. She was really walking away from him for the sake of his happiness.

***

Nava checked to make sure she was parked in front of the correct address. The fact that it was in the rear of the town homes confirmed it because King was always discreet when it came to his dealing. By the looks of the place, he was spending a pretty penny for it. She signaled for her friends to park and climbed out of the convertible. Diamond told her of a possible woman and that was the reason she knocked four times before pulling out the key she was given, Nava's heart began to race, knowing she'd find a shit load of cash and drugs. This was definitely worth the wait. "Let's hurry up and do this," she told them before pushing the door inward, and to make sure she was the first to find the cash, she told them, "Y'all check and see what's in the storage space over there." She tossed the gold-toothed guy the key.

Nava made her way through the town home and once she was sure she was alone, she smiled. She'd been playing the game a while and knew the rewards her diligence would bring. She knew if she only stayed down and played the game without rules, she would eventually win, and today was that day. She was in the second room when she saw it. The three-foot-tall safe on the side of the dresser brought a smile to her face. "Shit," she whispered, realizing she wasn't given the combination. To her surprise, it opened after she entered King's social security number. It was the same code he used for the safe she was said to have robbed the first time she left.

Stacks and stacks of bills lined each row and she knew she was looking at the most money she'd seen in her life. "Hey!" she yelled, but her excitement muted her voice. "Hey!" she managed a second time. "I'm in the back!" Nava closed her eyes and shook her head, praying like hell this wasn't a dream. "Motherfuckers, I'm—" Nava turned, saw the familiar face. "Diamond?"

Diamond smiled. Her hair was pulled back into a braided ponytail and covered with a Dallas Cowboys fitted cap. She pointed a Glock with an extended clip at Nava. "I just had to come make sure everything went right."

"Um, I-I told you I would take care of it."

"Thanks."

"What's the gun for?" Nava frowned.

"Oh, my bad." Diamond smiled and told her, "That's a lot of money."

"Yeah, huh?" Nava looked past Diamond, hoping to see her friends.

"Were those your friends outside?" Diamond turned slightly, while pointing behind her.

"Um, yeah. They've been rolling with me since the beginning." Nava watched Diamond with question. It was definitely something different about her. Something edgier.

"Since you called yourself doing something for me, I had to return the favor." Diamond stepped into the room, allowing two other guys to enter.

Nava's brows raised, but it wasn't until she saw the short balding guy enter thather mouth flew open. "Daddy?"

Sergio Munez stared at his daughter. He'd finally caught up with the one person that had caused him so much pain, so much grief and so much money.

"Ah, La'Navia, you are no daughter of mine."

"Daddy, I—"

"No, La'Navia. You no longer matter to me."

Diamond stood and watched the father-daughter exchange. He'd told her bits and piece of his reasons for searching for his disowned daughter but when hearing that Nava was behind the death of two of Sergio's most trusted men and his only son—her brother—Diamond wasn't about to turn her back on him and when he spoke of the two hundred and fifty thousand dollars' bounty he placed on her head particularly and the heads of her goons in general, Diamond couldn't refuse. Nava had her own father robbed numerous times, but it wasn't until the death of Sergio Muñoz's only son did he realize his daughter and her companions had to be dealt with and it was her most recent attempt to jack his

DPW shipment that pointed him in her direction. And, he'd been waiting for this moment for a while.

"Daddy, please, let me explain." Nava looked from Diamond to the man standing in front of her.

"You killed your own brother for crumbs, Nava. You wrecked our lives while feeding a habit You—"

"You always chose him over me!" Nava cried. "You always chose him."

"You had it all, Nava, the life many envied, the love of kings and queens. But, your jealousy separated us. Your jealousy had no bounds and the life you chose for yourself has led you to this." Sergio looked over at Diamond. You're more of a daughter than she ever was, Young Diamond."

It finally came to Nava. "This bitch set me up?"

"Take your money and go, Young Diamond. I need to be alone with my . . ." The words never came, but Diamond knew exactly what was being said.

Diamond turned, followed Sergio's men through the town home and closed her eyes when she stepped over the two bodies that lay at the door. This was what she was willing to do for the people she loved and now that the cards were in place, she could have no regrets and as always, Chanel McClendon wouldn't.

Nicole Goosby

EPILOGUE

Somolia's grand opening was bigger than she imagined. Not only were there people lined outside to see the ceremony, but many had come to see how good the beauticians were as well. Diamond paid for the live entertainment and Buddy made sure the kids had fun as well. The free ice cream was a favorite among them and this was a moment she was hoping would last.

"I want to thank all of you for helping me in this event." Somolia wiped her eyes with the napkins Buddy gave her. He'd been there since the beginning and had yet to leave her side.

"Don't start that shit, Somolia. Ya fat ass ain't even made a dollar yet and you crying," Datrina spoke, seeing her friend start her act.

"This is your day, Somolia, this is your day." Silvia stood next to KP and Raymond. She knew exactly what her friend was going through. She'd been there a couple of times herself.

"Are we going to stand out here all day or what?" Diamond stood next to King while waiting for Somolia to finish with her theatrics.

"Y'all just leave the woman alone and let her say what she's got to say." Chris was holding his girl from behind, thinking of ways to say what he'd been wanting to say for a while.

Buddy grabbed Somolia's hand, spun her to where she faced him and looked back to Camille, who nodded approvingly. "Somolia—" he began.

"Aw, shit," Datrina chimed in, seeing the obvious. Chris squeezed her.

Buddy continued, "I know we haven't known each other that long, but since I've been knowing you, I haven't been able to think of anything or anyone else. You're the reason I'm able to re-evaluate my life with you." Buddy pulled the small box from his pocket and opened it, displaying the three-carat diamond ring for all to see. "Somolia Rhodes, will you marry me?"

Somolia froze, looked back at Silvia and Datrina and covered her mouth with her hands. "Are you serious, Buddy?"

"As I'll ever be."

"Bitch, say yes!" Datrina yelled. She began wiping the tears that formed in the corners of her eyes.

"Yes, yes, yesss, Buddy. I will marry you." Somolia jumped into his arms. The people that gathered began clapping.

"I'm happy for you, Somolia. I really am." Datrina dabbed at the corners of her eyes and turned to face Chris. "I—"

Chris was on one knee when she faced him. This wasn't exactly the way he wanted to do it, but Buddy had given him the courage he needed. "Bae, you have been my everything for—"

"Yes!" Datrina pulled his head to her. Yeah," she told him without being asked.

Diamond smiled at the scene before her. Her heart lightened. She'd been wanting this for her friends and after the talk she and Chris had, she knew it was just a matter of time. She even picked out the ring he was proposing with and with the money Sergio gave her, Chris owed nothing. Diamond was just about to say something when she looked over at King. "Don't do it, King."

"What?"

"Don't even try it. I'm telling you." She eyed him, making sure he understood.

"Ain't shit romantic about standing outside a salon."

"Diamond, you tripping." King pulled her to him and kissed her forehead.

"I love you and all, but that's not going to cut it."

King shook his head, glanced in Camille's direction and shrugged. He knew exactly what he wanted to say, but now that Diamond had spoken her mind about it, he'd save it for another time—a more romantic setting.

***

Camille was following Diamond into the shop when she stopped her. They hadn't talked since that morning a week ago and Camille was fine with that. She really didn't know what happened or who it happened to. But, seeing Diamond in good spirits was enough for her, and the smile on her face showed her there was something she'd been wanting to tell her. "What's up, Diamond?"

"I believe this belongs to you. Diamond handed her a set of keys. "My brother said something about a deal the two of you had."

"A deal?"

"Yep."

Camille looked down at the keys in her hand, expecting to see keys to the Camaro he'd rebuilt. The very one she took a liking to, but instead was looking at house keys. "These are house keys, Diamond."

"Yeah, four-million-dollar house keys." Diamond shrugged and said, "Dell won't be needing it anymore."

Camille looked from Diamond to Silvia and Raymond. They nodded in agreement. This was the same house she wanted for herself. This as the dream house Dell was trying to sell her and it was now here. "I'm going to have to go thank Antonio personally."

"No need. He'll be out in a couple of weeks," Raymond assured her with a smile."

"Really?"

They all nodded. "Really."

***

Dell avoided his associates as best he could and when hearing the doorbell chime for the third time, he decided to tell them what they could do with their threats. The deal they made had been paid and he wasn't about to be extorted any longer. He walked through the marble foyer, saw two guys standing on the other side through opaque windows and swung open the door. He frowned when seeing faces he hadn't seen before. "Can I help you, officers?"

"Lindell Proctor?"

"That's me."

Dell's eyes followed the officers' hands. He watched as one of them unbuckled handcuffs.

"You're under arrest for the murders of both Scott Pinland and Joel Reed." Dell was spun around and pulled out of his home. "Murders?"

"You have the right to remain silent."

Dell's mind clouded as did his vision and his hearing. This was the game they played for his reluctance to pay a debt he'd paid many times over. This was repercussion for his climbing into bed with snakes.

From the rear of the patrol car, Dell could only watch his life fall apart. He watched as they slowly pulled away from his reasons for playing the game, from the very thing he wanted more than anything. Position. His rise to power and wealth had been because he played without rules. He'd played against the very ones that put him in position. He'd played the game against Antonio McClendon.

***

Antonio smiled when writing the last chapter in the book he had yet to title. Things had come together faster than they would have, had he not taken the reins off of his sister and that was a decision he had to make before any.

He'd learned of Dell's role in his incarceration long ago, but wanted to be sure. He needed to be sure, because Dell had become more than just an associate. He'd become family. He became that person he entrusted with all he owned and he eventually became the person to betray him for it. When Dell saw Antonio, he saw power and that was all it took for him to want the same, not knowing there was only one way to obtain it. Despite all that Dell did and cost him, Antonio still felt for his friend but when looking at the transformation it brought about in his sister—Chanel McClendon—he'd do it all again. In the course of it all, his little sister found something priceless, something he'd been wanting for her for the longest. Not only did she find her King. His Diamond had finally found love.

218

A Drug King and His Diamond 3

The End

To receive a FREE CATALOG, send a SASE along with three stamps to:
Lock Down Publications
Po Box 944
Stockbridge, Ga 30281

Submission Guideline.

Submit the first three chapters of your completed manuscript to ldpsubmissions@gmail.com, subject line: Your book's title. The manuscript must be in a .doc file and sent as an attachment. Document should be in Times New Roman, double spaced and in size 12 font. Also, provide your synopsis and full contact information. If sending multiple submissions, they must each be in a separate email.

Have a story but no way to send it electronically? You can still submit to LDP/Ca$h Presents. Send in the first three chapters, written or typed, of your completed manuscript to:

LDP: Submissions Dept
Po Box 870494
Mesquite, Tx 75187

DO NOT send original manuscript. Must be a duplicate.

Provide your synopsis and a cover letter containing your full contact information.

Thanks for considering LDP and Ca$h Presents.

<u>Coming Soon from Lock Down Publications/Ca$h Presents</u>

BOW DOWN TO MY GANGSTA

By **Ca$h**

TORN BETWEEN TWO

By **Coffee**

BLOOD STAINS OF A SHOTTA **III**

By **Jamaica**

STEADY MOBBIN II

By **Marcellus Allen**

BLOOD OF A BOSS **V**

By **Askari**

LOYAL TO THE GAME **IV**

By **T.J. & Jelissa**

A DOPEBOY'S PRAYER **II**

By **Eddie "Wolf" Lee**

IF LOVING YOU IS WRONG… **III**

LOVE ME EVEN WHEN IT HURTS

By **Jelissa**

TRUE SAVAGE **V**

By **Chris Green**

BLAST FOR ME **III**

ROTTEN TO THE CORE **III**

By **Ghost**

ADDICTIED TO THE DRAMA **III**

By **Jamila Mathis**

LIPSTICK KILLAH **III**

CRIME OF PASSION **II**

By **Mimi**

WHAT BAD BITCHES DO **III**

By **Aryanna**

THE COST OF LOYALTY **II**

By **Kweli**

SHE FELL IN LOVE WITH A REAL ONE **II**

By **Tamara Butler**

LOVE SHOULDN'T HURT **III**

By **Meesha**

CORRUPTED BY A GANGSTA **III**

By **Destiny Skai**

A GANGSTER'S CODE III

By **J-Blunt**

KING OF NEW YORK II

By **T.J. Edwards**

CUM FOR ME **IV**

By **Ca$h & Company**

WHO SHOT YA II

Renta

Nicole Goosby

LAST OF A DYING BREED

BLOOD STAINS OF A SHOTTA I & II

By **Jamaica**

LOYAL TO THE GAME

LOYAL TO THE GAME II

LOYAL TO THE GAME III

By **TJ & Jelissa**

BLOODY COMMAS I & II

SKI MASK CARTEL I II & III

KING OF NEW YORK

By **T.J. Edwards**

IF LOVING HIM IS WRONG…I & II

By **Jelissa**

WHEN THE STREETS CLAP BACK I & II III

By **Jibril Williams**

A DISTINGUISHED THUG STOLE MY HEART I II & III

LOVE SHOULDN'T HURT I II

By **Meesha**

A GANGSTER'S CODE I & II

By J-Blunt

PUSH IT TO THE LIMIT

By **Bre' Hayes**

BLOOD OF A BOSS **I, II, III & IV**

By **Askari**

THE STREETS BLEED MURDER **I, II & III**

THE HEART OF A GANGSTA I II& III

By **Jerry Jackson**

CUM FOR ME

CUM FOR ME 2

CUM FOR ME 3

An **LDP Erotica Collaboration**

BRIDE OF A HUSTLA **I II & II**

THE FETTI GIRLS **I, II& III**

CORRUPTED BY A GANGSTA I & II

By **Destiny Skai**

WHEN A GOOD GIRL GOES BAD

By **Adrienne**

A GANGSTER'S REVENGE **I II III & IV**

THE BOSS MAN'S DAUGHTERS

THE BOSS MAN'S DAUGHTERS II

THE BOSSMAN'S DAUGHTERS III

THE BOSSMAN'S DAUGHTERS IV

THE BOSS MAN'S DAUGHTERS **V**

A SAVAGE LOVE **I & II**

BAE BELONGS TO ME

A HUSTLER'S DECEIT I, II

WHAT BAD BITCHES DO I, II

By **Aryanna**

A KINGPIN'S AMBITON

A KINGPIN'S AMBITION **II**

I MURDER FOR THE DOUGH

By **Ambitious**

TRUE SAVAGE

TRUE SAVAGE II

TRUE SAVAGE **III**

TRUE SAVAGE **IV**

By **Chris Green**

A DOPEBOY'S PRAYER

By **Eddie "Wolf" Lee**

THE KING CARTEL **I, II & III**

By **Frank Gresham**
THESE NIGGAS AIN'T LOYAL **I, II & III**
By **Nikki Tee**
GANGSTA SHYT **I II &III**
By **CATO**
THE ULTIMATE BETRAYAL
By **Phoenix**
BOSS'N UP **I , II & III**
By **Royal Nicole**
I LOVE YOU TO DEATH
By Destiny J
I RIDE FOR MY HITTA
I STILL RIDE FOR MY HITTA
By **Misty Holt**
LOVE & CHASIN' PAPER
By **Qay Crockett**
TO DIE IN VAIN
By **ASAD**
BROOKLYN HUSTLAZ
By **Boogsy Morina**
BROOKLYN ON LOCK I & II
By **Sonovia**
GANGSTA CITY
By **Teddy Duke**
A DRUG KING AND HIS DIAMOND I & II III
A DOPEMAN'S RICHES
By Nicole Goosby
TRAPHOUSE KING I II & III
By **Hood Rich**
LIPSTICK KILLAH **I, II**

CRIME OF PASSION
By **Mimi**
STEADY MOBBN'
By **Marcellus Allen**
WHO SHOT YA
Renta

<u>BOOKS BY LDP'S CEO, CA$H</u>

<u>TRUST IN NO MAN</u>

<u>TRUST IN NO MAN 2</u>

<u>TRUST IN NO MAN 3</u>

<u>BONDED BY BLOOD</u>

<u>SHORTY GOT A THUG</u>

<u>THUGS CRY</u>

<u>THUGS CRY 2</u>

<u>THUGS CRY 3</u>

<u>TRUST NO BITCH</u>

<u>TRUST NO BITCH 2</u>

<u>TRUST NO BITCH 3</u>

<u>TIL MY CASKET DROPS</u>

<u>RESTRAINING ORDER</u>

<u>RESTRAINING ORDER 2</u>

<u>IN LOVE WITH A CONVICT</u>

<u>Coming Soon</u>

BONDED BY BLOOD 2

BOW DOWN TO MY GANGSTA

A Drug King and His Diamond 3

CPSIA information can be obtained
at www.ICGtesting.com
Printed in the USA
LVHW081525200620
658105LV00004B/258